OTTO AND THE SS

'He w poon.'

n saying

Also by Leo Kessler

The *SS Assault Regiment Wotan* Series
SS PANZER BATTALION
DEATH'S HEAD
CLAWS OF STEEL
GUNS AT CASSINO
THE DEVIL'S SHIELD
HAMMER OF THE GODS
FORCED MARCH
BLOOD AND ICE
THE SAND PANTHERS
COUNTER-ATTACK
PANZER HUNT
SLAUGHTER GROUND
HELLFIRE
FLASHPOINT
CAULDRON OF BLOOD
SCHIRMER'S HEADHUNTERS
WHORES OF WAR
SCHIRMER'S DEATH LEGION

The *Stormtroop* Series
STORMTROOP
BLOOD MOUNTAIN
VALLEY OF THE ASSASSINS
RED ASSAULT
HIMMLER'S GOLD
FIRE OVER KABUL
WAVE OF TERROR

The *Otto Stahl* Series
OTTO'S PHONEY WAR
OTTO'S BLITZKRIEG!
OTTO AND THE REDS
OTTO AND THE YANKS

The Sea Wolves Series
SINK THE SCHARNHORST!
DEATH TO THE DEUTSCHLAND

Also:

As Klaus Konrad
The Russian Series
FIRST BLOOD
MARCH ON MOSCOW
FRONT SWINE

Leo Kessler

Otto Stahl 5
Otto and the SS

Futura
Macdonald & Co
London & Sydney

A Futura Book

First published in Great Britain in 1983
by Futura Publications, a Division of
Macdonald & Co (Publishers) Ltd
London & Sydney

ISBN 0 7088 2376 9

Filmset, printed and bound in Great Britain by
Hazell Watson & Viney Limited,
Member of the BPCC Group,
Aylesbury, Bucks

Futura Publications
A Division of
Macdonald & Co (Publishers) Ltd
Maxwell House
74 Worship Street
London EC2A 2EN
A BPCC plc Company

Publisher's Introduction

Herr Otto Stahl, it appears, has done it again!

Frankly, when he turned up in London with his biographer, Herr Leo Kessler, offering to sell the details of the 'last great secret of World War Two,' as he put it, we were dubious. Virtually every other day, publishers' offices are besieged with elderly, white-haired gents such as Otto, offering to do the same. Forty years after it all ended, there seem to be a devil of a lot of 'last secrets' around!

Yet on the basis of the evidence that Herr Stahl has shown us, it appears that his astonishing claim is true. Indeed, after we had listened to Herr Stahl's astounding disclosures of what happened in Paris in December, 1944, we felt constrained to warn him that his life might be at risk if we published. Never a man to disdain a cliché, Herr Stahl merely snorted, 'Publish and be damned!'

So we have published. Now it is up to the historians of the 20th century to weigh and assess the impact of his startling disclosures on the course of post-World War Two history. For it would appear that for the last six months of that war, the five-million-strong Allied Army in Western Europe was led by a superannuated actor who had achieved the exalted rank of second-lieutenant! Not only that, astonishing as it is: that same ex-actor, 'the pride of New England summer stock,' as he was wont to call himself before he became Supreme Commander, went on to become the first commander of NATO, and then *President of the United States – for eight long years!*

So here it is – 'the last great secret of World War Two,' and a book which we are *proud* to publish. Now that the truth has been told at last, perhaps that other ex-actor in the White House might be magnanimous enough to set the record straight officially, before it is too late . . .

N. Chapman,
Publisher, London, 1982

A MISSION IS PROPOSED

'Buy combs, lad, there are lousy times ahead.'

The sayings of Otto Stahl

Adolf Hitler farted yet again.

Next to him, his tall, cadaverous servant, Heinz Linge, blanched. The Führer was at it again. Even now that he was dying, he was still terrified of getting fat. 'A leader must be as lean and tough as a wolf,' he had always proclaimed – hence the laxatives and vegetables with which he had stuffed himself all through his political career. 'Real old fart food!' Linge had cursed more than once to his fat Viennese lady-cook. 'God in heaven, sometimes I wish I were at the front and not here with that stink! At least they don't use poison gas there!'

Holding his breath, Linge unscrewed the cap of the bottle of Morell's anti-gas pills and offered one to his master.

Slowly the man who had once been dictator of the greatest empire Europe had ever seen sat up in his chair, face pale and puffy, and with a violently trembling hand, accepted and swallowed the pill, his stomach rumbling noisily the while, as if in the grip of a great wind-storm.

'Linge,' croaked Hitler, holding his shaking left arm steady, 'bring in Skorzeny now. I think my little, er, affliction is over for the time being.'

'*Jawohl, mein Führer*,' snapped the tall manservant, who wore the black uniform of a full colonel in the SS, and hurriedly fled from the fetid room. As soon as he was outside, he thrust the bottle of Eau-de-Cologne that he always carried first up one nostril and then the other, drawing in the powerful cleansing odour gratefully, like a drug addict taking his first fix of the day.

The huge man standing in the corner, whose scar-covered face looked like the work of a drunken butcher armed with a blunt tin-opener, stared curiously. It *did* make rather a peculiar sight: an ashen-faced colonel of the SS sticking a bottle of Cologne up his nose.

'Are you feeling a little faint, sir?' ventured the big man, in the soft, warm accents of middle-class Vienna.

'*Faint*,' Linge cried angrily. 'I'm shitting well dy—'

The words died on his lips as he recognized the huge man in the grey uniform with the Knight's Cross dangling from his throat, his chest bedecked with awards and decorations. It was Skorzeny, of course – Otto Skorzeny, head of the SS's undercover Hunting Commando. Everyone knew *his* ugly mug, for in '43, the 'Poison Dwarf'[1] had splashed it over the front page of every paper in the Reich after he had rescued Mussolini from captivity in Italy. Recently he'd pulled off another bold *coup*, kidnapping the playboy son of the Hungarian dictator, Admiral Horthy, by smuggling him out of Budapest in a carpet. In this way he had forced his father to stop all peace talks with the Russians and remain in the war on Germany's side. Yes, everybody knew Otto Skorzeny.

'Why, my dear Skorzeny,' said Linge, all gentle charm now, and added the Viennese greeting '*Küss die Hand*' for good measure – though in fact he hadn't the least desire to kiss the Austrian's paw, which looked like a bunch of hairy pork sausages.

'*Küss die Hand*,' echoed Skorzeny, and straightened his tunic in readiness for his audience with the All-Highest. Pirouetting round on the tips of his highly polished riding boots like a grey-clad ballet-dancer, he perused his image in the long mirror on the wall opposite.

Hurriedly, Linge strode across to the pirouetting giant and with the trained, expert fingers of a professional valet, swiftly adjusted the Austrian's decorations, giving his

[1] Nickname for Dr Goebbels, the undersized, club-footed head of the German Ministry of Propaganda

Knight's Cross a light tug, so that it sat directly in the middle of the collar.

'Just try not to move your head too violently, my dear Skorzeny,' he cautioned, 'or it'll move out of position, which would be a shame. The Führer is a stickler for detail, as you know. Now . . .' And he raised his arms like a conductor about to commence a concert.

Skorzeny recognized the signal. He dropped to his heels.

'Ready,' he barked.

'One . . . Two . . . *Three* . . .'

Bringing down his arms as if to lead the orchestra into the first bars of some great symphony, walking backwards as he did so, Linge drew the giant after him, pausing only to throw open the great doors and bellow at the top of his voice in the approved style; '*Mein Führer . . . Obersturmbannführer Skorzeny!*'

Skorzeny stalked in, hat clutched to his right side, narrowly missed stumbling over the Führer's pet alsatian bitch, Blondi, stamped to attention and barked, '*Heil, mein Führer!*' at the stooped figure hunched in the big chair opposite him.

Slowly and with an obvious effort, Hitler levered up his right arm and croaked '*Heil!*' He hadn't even the strength to shoo away Blondi, who had squatted down in the fashion of bitches and was beginning to urinate on the giant's gleaming right boot.

Standing at the door, a long-suffering Linge shook his head in despair. If it wasn't the boss farting all the time, it was that wretched Alsatian bitch pissing all over the place! For a chap who had served in some of the finest households in the Reich, it was sometimes downright embarrassing. He often wondered if his high rank of colonel in the SS justified the torture to which the Führer submitted him; the pay wasn't much to write home about either.

'At ease, my dear chap . . . At ease,' croaked Hitler, and reaching over, took an opium pill from one of the numerous pill-boxes on the little table next to his chair, to ease the pain in his poor gas-rent stomach. Each day he swallowed sixty or more.

Gratefully, the Viennese giant moved his right foot out of the puddle. Blondi, disturbed thus, wandered away to squat in the corner, from which position she eyed the room, wondering where she might relieve herself next. Linge cursed under his breath. They could fill a sodding reservoir with the amount of urine that animal passed every twenty-four hours.

'Well done, Skorzeny,' said Hitler, indicating the chair opposite his own. 'Sit down, my dear chap and tell me about this, er, Operation Mickey Mouse of yours in Hungary.'

For the next few minutes, Skorzeny described how he had kidnapped the young playboy Horthy, whose nickname was Mickey, and how he had bundled him out of Budapest's Citadel. Listening, Hitler laughed in a pathetic fashion. A watching Linge noted that a little colour had returned to the Führer's faded cheeks, and he stepped back a little apprehensively, hoping that the colour was due to Skorzeny's tale and didn't herald another attack of wind.

Finally the giant ran out of words and, unsettled a little by the sudden silence, rose as if to go.

Hitler shook his head. 'Stay awhile, my dear Skorzeny. I have something very important to say to you.'

Skorzeny sat down again and waited. Behind him, Blondi had risen and was sauntering idly over to the little antique table which the Duke of Windsor had given to the Führer during his visit of 1939. Linge didn't intervene. After all, it was English, and anything English deserved to be pissed on. They should have pissed on Churchill back in '40 while they still had the chance; perhaps if they had, they wouldn't have been in the mess they were in now. He sighed. Life at the top was hard.

'Skorzeny,' said Hitler, and for the first time this cold October morning there was enthusiasm in his voice. 'I have made a momentous decision.'

Skorzeny tensed.

Hitler let him wait for a moment, then continued: 'I am taking the offensive once again, Skorzeny.'

'The offensive, mein Führer,' Skorzeny breathed. 'Where?'

Again, Hitler paused dramatically. Linge looked out at the fog through the window. It was another grey Autumn day, as boring as the present conversation. He must have witnessed this dramatic little scene a good score of times already. It was the same each time: the gentle beginning, the dramatic announcement, the pause, the astonishment of the listener . . . All week long, the generals and field marshals from every front in the Reich had been trooping in and out of this same room to be told the great secret, leaving starry-eyed and enthusiastic, muttering that the 'Führer's genius' had returned yet again – hoping naturally that Bormann[1] might hear the flattering comment and pass it on to Hitler afterwards.

'The Ardennes, Skorzeny, the Ardennes,' Hitler said finally, while Blondi squatted there, seemingly sinking in a sea of warm, yellow urine.

'The Ardennes,' Skorzeny breathed. 'Why, mein Führer, that is pure genius, if I may say so. It is the most weakly defended part of the whole Allied front and snowbound in winter – so the enemy will never suspect that we would use it for an offensive! And most of the troops the Amis have stationed there are from unblooded "green" divisions.' Skorzeny gasped for air, eyes gleaming with excitement. 'My Leader, who but you, Germany's saviour, could have thought up such a brilliant scheme in this, the Reich's hour of need! *Es ist genial!*'

'Heaven, arse and cloudburst!' Linge cursed under his breath, 'he's going to kiss the Führer's arse in a minute!' For his part, Hitler looked down at his trembling fingers with due modesty. Blondi peed on.

For the next few minutes, Hitler explained to the

[1] Hitler's secretary and 'grey eminence'.

awestruck giant how he and his staff had discussed various plans for the offensive in the West for weeks, until finally *he* had decided on the Ardennes. Then he looked straight at Skorzeny, using his old trick of trying to mesmerize his listener into total submission by means of eye-to-eye contact. Often Linge had caught him standing in front of the mirror in his bedroom practising the look, raising his jaw slightly or lowering it to achieve a better effect, his dark eyes blazing with fake intensity. On one occasion, which Linge had witnessed, the Führer's mistress had entered the room stark naked and watched him for five long minutes, and Hitler hadn't even noticed. Not so Linge: he'd had to rush out of the room, driven to a frenzy of lust by the sight of Eva Braun's naked body.

'Now, Skorzeny,' Hitler said at last, 'I have a role – a *vital* role – in this new operation for you and your men of the Hunting Commando.'

'Sir?'

'I am giving you unlimited power to set up a whole brigade of English – and American-speaking soldiers.'

'A whole brigade!' Skorzeny echoed in disbelief. At present he commanded exactly a hundred and fifty men, and most of them were only 'booty Germans'.[1]

'Yes, three thousand men, who will be trained by yourself. You speak fluent English, I take it?'

'Yes, I am speaking English good,' Skorzeny ventured wildly. He beamed at the Führer, delighted to find how quickly his school English had come back to him.

Linge gave a soft moan of dismay and willed Blondi to piss on the stupid giant's other boot.

'As I was saying then, Skorzeny, you will train your brigade to masquerade as Americans. They will operate behind US lines, wearing American uniforms and driving American vehicles. Their task will be to spread rumours, give false orders, breed confusion and panic, seize the key

[1] Name given to citizens of the German-occupied East, whose forefathers in the distant past had once been of German origin.

bridges across the River Meuse which our panzers will need in due course, *and* – '

At this point the Führer paused and then to Linge's surprise, leant forward to whisper something in the big Austrian's ear; it was almost as if he didn't trust his valet of these last eleven years to keep a secret.

Linge frowned and forgot Blondi. He strained hard, but could hear nothing. All the same, he could see the effect the Führer's words were having on Skorzeny. His face blanched, then flushed a deep red. The exultant look disappeared from his eyes to be replaced by one of utter terror. Suddenly the giant's chest began to heave, as if he were in throes of some almost unbearable passion.

Linge's frown deepened even more. What *had* the Führer said to him to affect him like this?

Finally the Führer leaned back in his chair, a satisfied smile on his face. For a moment, it seemed, even his gas pains were forgotten.

Skorzeny, however, looked as if he was about to ask a question, but was clearly experiencing some difficulty in expressing himself. His big head was twisted to one side as if he were being strangled, his face flushing a deep scarlet. In the end he abandoned the attempt and instead drew a thick finger across his throat, giving the Führer a worried look.

Hitler nodded hid head eagerly. 'Yes, my dear Skorzeny, that is *exactly* what I mean!'

Skorzeny gulped audibly.

Linge sucked his teeth. Obviously the Führer wanted the big Austrian to kill someone – but who in three devils' name could it be?

So intrigued was he by the little scene taking place in dumb show before his eyes that Linge completely failed to notice that Blondi had squatted down and was pissing on *his* boots. By the time he realized, it was, of course, far too late to stop her. Moments later Otto Skorzeny was gone, taking that dread, unspoken mission with him, and Linge was squelching to the door to admit the next visitor. . .

DAY ONE : FRIDAY, DECEMBER 15th, 1944

'Sin begets sin'

The Talmud

It was bitterly cold. The black GI guarding the roadblock stamped his feet in the frozen snow, burying his face even deeper in the collar of his greatcoat. Brother, was he looking forward to his relief! It was colder out here than a well-digger's ass!

Behind him in the blacked-out houses which lined the bank of the River Sauer, a door flew open. Yellow light sliced the darkness. There was a snatch of tinny accordion music, the beat of drums, a burst of coarse laughter. The sentry frowned ruefully. They'd be the whores who catered for the whiteys – black GIs had to go all the way to Lux City to get laid in one of the 'Colored Only' cathouses that the US Army had set up for its black soldiers.

The door closed, and once more all was silence – heavy, brooding and a little frightening. The black soldier turned and stared at the massive outline of the Ferschweiler Plateau across the river, its fir trees silhouetted stark black against the silver light of the moon and looking like a regiment of spike-helmeted Prussian guards on the march. Somewhere up there were the Krauts, but as usual there was no sign of them; there hadn't been ever since September, when the US Army had first reached the river. They were there all right, but he'd never seen a single one of them in all the three months that he'd been stationed here. He stamped his frozen feet once more and thanked God he'd been sent to what the other GIs called the 'Ghost Front'. It might be damned cold, but it was sure better than having your balls shot off up north around Aachen.

Time passed leadenly. A flying bomb heading for

Antwerp or perhaps even London chugged overhead, sounding for all the world like a two-stroke motor-bike. The black soldier clasped his helmet more firmly on his cropped skull and stared upwards. He could see its fiery red trail as it headed westwards, bearing its ton of high explosive – sudden death for some poor bastards in an hour or so. Over in the direction of Lux City, the searchlights flicked on. For a few moments they poked probing stiff white fingers into the sky. But as the bomb continued to plod purposefully westwards beyond the city, they flickered out again. Lux City was safe for the night; let somebody else worry about the buzz bomb.

The black soldier looked at the green glowing dial of his watch. Another ten minutes to go, then he'd hit the pot-bellied stove and the java and try and get some warmth back into his frozen, skinny black body before he turned in for the rest of the night. He licked his frost-cracked lips in anticipation. Hell, that'd be better than laying some whitey whore in Lux City at ten bucks a throw!

But it was not to be. That black sentry posted at the remote roadblock was not fated to enjoy his coffee and bed that night or any other night, for that matter. For exactly five minutes before he was due to be relieved, a dark, dripping figure detached itself from the shadows of the ruined bridge which spanned the Sauer. Almost noiselessly, the dark figure, crouching low, crept towards the unsuspecting sentry. At the very last moment, the sentry heard the soft crunch of feet on the frozen snow. He turned, startled, already trying to unsling the carbine slung over his skinny shoulder. Too late!

The dark figure bounded forward. The terrified GI caught a fleeting glimpse of a wolfish, animal face clad in what appeared to be a wet rubber hood. Next instant, the gloved hand clamped over his mouth, stiffling his scream of fear. The dark figure in the gleaming rubber suit grunted hard. The sentry's spine arched like a taut bow as the cruel blade slid into his stomach. Desperately he tried to wrench himself free from that vice-like grip. To no avail. The knife flashed silver and red again – and again. The sentry writhed in the assassin's arms as if in the throes of sexual passion. The stranger gave one last animal grunt and thrust the knife into the sentry's savaged stomach a final time. Suddenly the GI went limp. Gently, very gently, the stranger lowered the dead body to the snow, the blood immediately staining it pink.

For a long moment the stranger crouched there, head cocked to one side, acutely aware of every faint sound, staring at the line of blacked-out riverside houses. But there was no sound save the distant strains of the *bal musette* music and the muted laughter of the Ami whores. The stranger sneered contemptuously. That was all the Amis were good for – bedding cheap, diseased prostitutes. It was only their overwhelming superiority in planes that had brought them so close to the holy soil of the Reich. But soon things would change. Yes, soon the whole cowardly pack of them, whores and all, would be running for their lives!

Keeping low, he ran down the bank, and flicked the light attached to his wetsuit on and off three times.

On the other side of the Sauer, a faint blue light returned his signal and a soft voice called across, '*All clear, Wolf*?'

'All clear, Jaguar. You can start bringing them across now!'

As he waited, listening to the faint sounds of the engineers on the far bank as they prepared to float the two jeeps across the river, he unzipped the frogman's suit supplied by Skorzeny's *Jagdkommando*, to reveal a US lieutenant's uniform, complete in every detail, right down to the blue combat infantryman's badge across the right pocket. He had hated the uniform of the enemy from the very start, but he knew that the wearing of it was vital if their mission was to succeed. Finally he slipped on the overseas cap, setting it at the jaunty angle favoured by the

Americans, and mockingly saluted the dead soldier sprawled out in the snow.

Turning, Wolf saw that already the first raft was touching the western bank of the Sauer, bearing the jeep and his two comrades 'Jaguar' and 'Lynx'. None of them knew each other's real names, though Wolf did happen to know that these two had once belonged to the SS – as he had himself. He hurried down the bank and helped wordlessly as the two of them, already dressed in the American uniforms taken from the dead of the November battles along the frontier, began to push the jeep up onto the road.

'Where's the other team?' Wolf snapped, looking at his two travelling companions, who like himself were blond, blue-eyed, hard-faced and exceedingly stiff, walking as if a poker had been thrust up their tunics.

'It's Seadog', snapped the one called Lynx. 'He forgot to strap on his wooden leg properly.'

'And Mex,' added Jaguar in the same stiff fashion. 'He stopped to take his sea-sick tablets – just in case.'

Wolf clapped a hand to his tall forehead in exasperation. 'Heavens above!' he cried. 'Whatever is the Fatherland coming to? Sending idiots like that on a mission of such importance!'

'At least they speak the language,' said Lynx.

Just then, the second raft appeared out of the silvery gloom, bearing the other team: Seadog, sitting in the back of the jeep, nursing a bottle of rum and grumbling to himself as usual; Mex, a distinguished-looking man with a theatrical air about him, who looked oddly out of place in the uniform of a corporal in the US Army; and at the wheel, Tex – blond, blue-eyed and cocky in what Wolf thought was a rather cheap, working-class sort of way.

Wolf hadn't cared for the fellow code-named Tex right from the start, and the private enquiries he had made about him had only increased his dislike. He had been startled by what he had found out. The chap's real name was Otto

Stahl – a case of *nomen es omen*[1] if ever there was one. Apparently, this Otto Stahl, together with his long-standing companion Count von der Weide, now code-named Mex, had been in espionage work ever since 1939, when they had successfully captured the Meuse bridges for the Wehrmacht. After that, they had been engaged in undercover ops behind enemy lines on virtually every front.[2] More than once they had been received by the Führer himself, an honour which Wolf himself hadn't yet enjoyed – though no doubt once he had successfully carried out this latest mission, he would achieve that life-long ambition.

Wolf was well aware that Otto had given great service to the holy cause of National Socialist Germany, yet in spite of it he couldn't take to the chap. He was simply too common and working-class, with his vulgar expressions and constant skirt-chasing. And Wolf strongly suspected, too, that Herr Otto Stahl's heart wasn't altogether in this mission. He didn't know why, but somehow or other he sensed it. Instinctively, his hand dropped stiffly to the knife with which he had killed the black GI . . .

'Come on, don't stand there like wet farts waiting to hit the thunderbox!' Otto's coarse Berlin tones came floating across to Wolf. 'Give us a hand! The Count here – I mean Mex – is going to toss up his cookies in a half a minute if we don't get off this water. Christ only knows how he ever crossed the Atlantic!'

Wolf hurriedly forgot his suspicions and together with Lynx and Jaguar, grabbed the rope and helped to heave the jeep up the slope, while Seadog hugged his precious bottle of rum tightly to his chest like a possessive mother nursing her first-born. Lightly Otto sprang from the seat of the jeep – and stopped in his tracks, his normally good-humoured face suddenly grim, as he saw the dead negro

[1] '*Stahl* is the German word for 'steel'.

[2] See *Otto's Phoney War*, *Otto's Blitzkrieg!*, *Otto and the Reds* and *Otto and the Yanks* for further details.

sprawled out in the snow, his stomach ripped to pieces, his blood already frozen solid on the snow.

Wolf followed the direction of his gaze with a stiff turn of his neck. 'Just a nigger,' he sneered.

Otto was about to say something, but the Count gave him a warning dig in his ribs. Even the Count, flamboyant and theatrical as he appeared, was shrewd enough to realize what dangerous company they found themselves in. The 'Zoo' – as Otto contemptuously called Wolf, Jaguar and Lynx behind their backs – had been hardened and brutalized by three years on the Russian front. In spite of their wooden appearance, they were killers, all three of them; and as the Count had warned Otto more than once since he and his young companion had become involved in this impossible mission, it wasn't wise to eat cherries with *that* trio. 'Otto, my dear boy,' he would say, 'they have the hangman's look about them.'

To which Otto would invariably reply, 'I wouldn't eat horseshit with that bunch.' Wisely, he tended to keep his normally loose tongue in check when they were about. It seemed safer that way – at least until they had reached the River Meuse and their mission was over. Then perhaps he could let off steam a bit . . .

'Are you ready, gentlemen?' asked the somewhat bewildered sergeant of engineers in charge of the rafts, obviously eager to get back to the German side of the river and allow these spies – for such he imagined them to be – to get on with their task.

'Ready,' snapped Wolf, taking his place next to Lynx in the first jeep. 'Tex?'

Otto nodded. Behind him, Seadog muttered, ''Bout time for another grog,' and belched. 'It's been a shitting long voyage this time.'

Turning to his comrades on the opposite bank of the river, the engineer sergeant flicked his flashlight on and off, and Wolf began to count to ten. Otto did the same. On the other side of the Sauer another blue light showed momentarily. Otto poised his forefinger and thumb on the ignition key, ready for what was to come.

Suddenly a cherry-red light flared high up on the cliff-like bank. A low, throaty cough.. An obscene howl, followed by another and another. Immediately the silence was torn apart as the first rocket screeched across the river, trailing a blaze of angry flame and sparks behind it. Wolf turned the key. The jeep's motor burst into noisy life, thick clouds of blue smoke spurting from the exhaust. Otto hesitated no longer. Already doors were being flung open all along the row of blacked-out houses opposite. Someone yelled an angry challenge. A woman screamed. A searchlight flicked on alarmingly. Otto turned his key. The jeep started first turn. Otto thrust home first gear and lurched forward.

'Ahoy there, me hearty!' Seadog protested. 'Nearly upset me grog!'

But Otto wasn't listening. Already he could hear the sound of booted feet running down the cobbled street which led out of the Luxembourg town. Wolf's jeep bounced over the dead body of the murdered GI. Otto swerved hastily to avoid it, and in the same instant a stream of tracer cut the air viciously. The slugs ripped through the dead body and continued along the road, kicking up a series of angry blue sparks. Otto bent low over the wheel and drove on regardless as wild firing erupted on all sides and half-naked Americans ran out into the street, dropping to their knees in the snow and shooting from the hip as they did so. A woman leaned out of an upstairs window, pendulous breasts hanging down below the sill, and screaming with rage, emptied a brimming chamber pot over the first racing jeep, drenching Jaguar, who, as bad luck would have it, had just happened to look up at that particular moment. Then, leaning out very dangerously and revealing that she was wearing nothing but black silk knickers, complete with red bows, she flung the empty chamber pot at the first jeep, where it struck Lynx's helmet and shattered in a burst of rose-coloured china, leaving the unfortunate SS officer dazed and confused, his lap full of wet shards. Frustrated beyond all measure, the woman shrieked as they raced on, '*Sales cons!*' – adding, presumably for the sake of international understanding, '*Dreckige Votzen! Deer-ty coonts!*'

'I say, Otto!' the Count remarked, hanging on for dear life as the jeep careened from side to side, belting up the hill that led out of the town. 'So *that*'s what it's called in English.' He repeated the word, savouring it idly for a moment, then dismissed it from his mind. After all, it was hardly an expression he would be needing again in a hurry.

Moments later, both jeeps had bounced over the hill and vanished into the night. The mission had commenced. Skorzeny's commandos were on their way . . .

As usual it had been the Count who had started it all. That Autumn, the three of them – the Count, Otto, and Otto's mother – had had almost a perfect set-up. Each morning Otto, looking suitably wan and handsome in his black market captain's uniform, Knight's Cross at his throat, would be pushed by his 'batman', the Count, to La Charité Hospital, attended by 'Schwester Klara', alias the Witch, looking surprisingly prim and proper in her Red Cross uniform, her normally bold, bloodshot eyes cast low and demure.

There, Otto would be wheeled into the consulting rooms of the chief surgeon, where discreet little presents – real bean coffee, tins of English corned beef, American cigarettes – would change hands, and Otto, watched sadly by the younger nurses, would emerge, bearing his daily 'certificate'. This entirely bogus document testified that he was suffering from an obscure nervous complaint brought about by wounds, and which gravely affected his 'nether limbs'. The consulting surgeon, in spite of his susceptibility to bribes, was surprisingly delicate and old-fashioned, but the euphemistic term 'nether limbs' didn't fool his nurses; they knew quite well that the blond young hero in the bath-chair had sacrificed his all for the Fatherland. He couldn't get his 'thing' up, they would whisper to each other as he passed, shaking their heads at such a terrible waste of German manhood.

Once Otto had been issued with his document, the day could really begin. Back at the Count's apartment the Witch would hurry into her 'working dress', a tight black silk affair that barely reached her skinny knees, strapping her flaccid breasts right up beneath her hairy chin, and taking out her teeth to give them a final polish with the scrubbing brush, before setting out to pound Berlin's pavements. More than once Otto had protested that they didn't really need the money – and besides, who would want an old bag like her? But always the Witch would give that secret smile of hers and say, 'My son, in the dark, all cats would be grey.' Then off she would trot to do her bit for 'our brave boys.'

Now it would be Otto's turn. Armed with his certificate and having made a remarkable recovery, he would set off through the smoking, ruined streets of the capital to meet 'Bare-Bosom Bertha', the source of his black market supplies, who, Otto calculated, would save him from active service and the rigours of the battlefield until the Allies finally won the war.

Bertha, the statuesque blonde wife of a high-ranking official in Goebbels' Ministry of Propaganda, derived her nickname from her impressive breasts, which she proudly displayed on every conceivable occasion. At parties – and the Poison Dwarf *always* seemed to be giving parties – she would often start removing her sweater before the drinks had been served. '*Must* you always show off your tired tits like that, Bertha?' Otto would complain.

But Bertha would give him her inane white-gleaming smile and declare, 'But Otto, *Liebster*, these people aren't bureaucrats, your boring civil servants. They're intellectuals, *artists*. They don't want polite chit-chat. They want something more unconventional.' And so saying she would stroke her ample white breasts lovingly, as if they were a pair of pet animals.

Still, at least she kept Otto and his companions well supplied with rations, ration-cards and the black market goods they needed to survive in Berlin in this Autumn of 1944 – and in bed she was unconventional enough. More than once, she had almost suffocated Otto with those huge breasts of hers, and after those mornings when she had suggested they they 'take a trip round the world,' he invariably felt that what he really needed was his bathchair.

Bertha's husband was a dour, frustrated former journalist attached to the Ministry of Propaganda, who specialized in sinking the British aircraft-carrier the *Ark Royal*. Since 1939, he had been torpedoing, mining, bombing her, according to the demands of the various branches of the Wehrmacht. Presently he was trying to find a way of having the long-suffering British warship shelled and sunk by a certain Lance-Corporal 'Beppo' Schmidt, who was a gun-layer in the beleaguered garrison of the French port of St Nazaire, one of the last German outposts in that country.

'It would be a terrific propaganda *coup*, Otto,' he explained to the latter, watching, but apparently not comprehending, as Bertha removed her sweater yet again, pausing with her hands raised in the air so that the entire company should get full benefit of the sight. 'Imagine the headlines: *Ark Royal*, sunk at last! Modest twenty-one-year-old declares all team work! Long live Germany!'

Bertha's husband never seemed worried by Otto's relationship with her. On the contrary, he would pat Otto's arm and remark, 'Try to keep the little woman happy, will you, my dear boy? I simply *can't* concern myself with . . . such matters when I'm *creating*.' And he would touch his fingertips to his high furrowed brow, eyes sad and set on some distant horizon.

And so Otto continued to concern himself with 'such

matters'; Bertha's husband 'created'; the Witch serviced her 'brave boys' – and all was well as could be expected in a war-torn world. Otto had even begun to make plans for post-war prosperity: he had started to buy quaint little watercolours painted by the Führer. At five Woodbines a time, they were remarkably cheap, and could be sold to Americans (great souvenir-hunters, as Otto knew) at exorbitant prices once the Allies had captured Berlin – which would be soon.

Until suddenly came the call to arms – that same dread summons which Otto Stahl had been assiduously avoiding – with little success, it must be admitted – since 1939. And once again it was the Count who landed him, as he put it in his own inimitable way, 'right up to his hooter in the crap!' Of course, he should have known the signs by now: the Count's heavy sighs, his long, brooding silences, the far-away look in his eyes – those suffering eyes which popped out of his fleshily handsome face like hard-boiled eggs. 'What *ennui*,' the Count would groan. 'What utter *ennui*! How I miss the Great Game, Otto . . . Life is so dull nowadays, isn't it, my dear boy!'

'*Dull!*' Otto would explode. 'Holy strawsack! *Dull*, you say! Every night the buck-teethed Tommies come and unload half a million tons of high explosive on top of us. Every day the Amis come at first light and do the shitting same. The Popovs are at our eastern frontier and the Allies are at our western – *and you call life dull!*' Otto would shake his head in exasperation and cry, 'Count, sometimes, I really do think you've gone *meschugge* – ain't got all yer cups in yer cupboard; got a little bird in yer upper storey that goes *tweet-tweet* – in other words, *you're nuts!*'

But the outbursts would have no effect on the Count, who would sigh deeply yet again and murmur in a sad, resigned way, 'But it isn't the same as the Great Game, my dear boy. Just isn't the same.'

Somehow or other the Count managed to lay his hands on a copy of the circular that was currently doing the rounds of Berlin's military units that Autumn – and he saw more in it than Otto did at the time. Unfortunately for Otto.

The circular had been signed by Field-Marshal Keitel of Hitler's staff and differed, so Otto thought, in no way from the thousands of other circulars floating around Germany in that year. It read:

> 'To all units of the Wehrmacht, Navy and Air Force and Waffen SS, with the exception of the fortresses on the Atlantic.
>
> The Führer has ordered the formation of special troops for employment in reconnaissance in the west. Strength: approx. two battalions.
>
> All captured US uniforms, equipment and vehicles are to be surrendered to the Quartermaster-General's Office by all formations, including the Waffen SS. Volunteers are requested from all units. They must:
>
> (*a*) Be physically fit for special duties, intelligent and agile.
>
> (*b*) Be fully combat-trained.
>
> (*c*) Have a knowledge of English, especially the American dialect, and understand military terms in these tongues.
>
> This order is to be made to all units at once. Volunteers are to report to Obersturmbannführer Skorzeny at Friedenthal near Berlin.

'Well?' said Otto, after he had read it, handing it back to a suddenly coy Count. 'What am I supposed to do – crap in my cap?'

'How crude you are sometimes, Otto,' the Count chided him mildly. 'No, nothing of that sort.' He looked down at his feet, as if he didn't wish Otto to see the look in his eyes. 'I thought we . . . might . . . er, volunteer.'

'*Volunteer!*' Otto exploded, but the Count caught his arm urgently.

'It's obvious that Skorzeny is setting up some sort of

interrogation unit. You know – to infiltrate American POW camps in the Reich and pump the Americans for what can be gotten out of them. Completely safe, I should say. And besides, Friedenthal is only half an hour from Berlin by train.' He coughed discreetly. 'You could visit your . . . er, *paramour*, naturally.'

But Otto wasn't convinced. '*Paramour*, Count! Christ on a crutch, what century do you live in? You mean Miss-Tits-with-the-built-in-foxhole! No, Count, I don't think I'm ready for volunteering again at the present time, even though it does sound, I'll agree with you, a very cushy billet indeed . . .'

In the end it was the spate of police raids that began in Berlin towards the end of that October that forced Otto's hand. Suddenly the middle-aged bulls and their assistants, the 'chain-dogs' of the military police, were everywhere, banging on doors, sealing off streets, examining passes, filling the waiting trucks with scores of hangdog deserters and scared foreign workers living illegally in the capital. The rumours flew thick and fast, as the mythical 'General Grab-All' sent his minions scuttling back and forth through Berlin, weeding out every available man between sixteen and sixty. As a worried Otto remarked, 'Yer don't need a frigging crystal ball to know what's coming. The Greatest Captain of All Times' – he meant the Führer – 'is getting ready for another bash. He's looking for cannon-fodder again. Buy combs, lads – there are lousy times ahead!'

One morning, as October gave way to a freezing, fog-bound November, Otto and the Witch were just preparing to go their separate ways after the daily visit to the hospital, when there was a thunderous knock on the door below, and a harsh voice bellowed, 'Open up! Military police here! *Los! Aufmachen! Feldgendarmerie!*'

'Shit,' Otto cursed, 'it's the chain-dogs!'

'Oh, dear me,' quavered the Count, his plump face suddenly ashen. 'What *are* we going to do? They shoot deserters, you know.'

'Leave it to me, your Grace,' cackled the Witch – for she had her false teeth out and was busily cleaning them with scouring powder and a nail brush, as was her custom before she went off for 'service on the bedroom front,' as she proudly called her whoring activities.

'What you gonna do?' Otto asked hurriedly, frantically casting around the apartment for some means of escape if the worst came to the worst. Already he could hear the truck grinding up the street below in low gear and an anxious male voice crying, '*Razzia! Es ist ein Razzia!*'[1]

'Scare the shit out of them, that's what,' the Witch answered, pulling her black stockings up her beanpole legs and fastening them with red garters. 'I'm off!'

The Count gulped, and Otto shook his head in mock wonder. What a mother he had! She'd frighten the paint off a panzer the way she looked at this particular moment. 'Stay there, Count. I'm gonna see what the old bag's up to,' Otto commanded, and followed her out of the room, crouching in the shadows at the top of the stairs, as the hammering and shouting continued down below.

'The door's open, darlings!' the Witch cooed, striking up what she thought was a seductive pose at the foot of the stairs, black-clad drainpipe legs spread invitingly.

Just then the door flew open and the first chain-dog, a broad-shouldered brute with evil cross-eyes, staggered backwards, aghast. 'Oh, my God, Hans! What in three devils' name *is* it?'

The Witch cackled. 'You naughty boy! I bet you looked right up my knickers and saw the ace of spades!' And wagging a skinny forefinger at the gawping military policeman, she thrust out her stomach in hideous, obscene invitation. 'All you fellows are alike. Young bulls out to seduce innocent maidens.' She grinned at the cross-eyed one, revealing her toothless gums. 'But then every one of us, man and maid, has to make sacrifices these days. Won't

[1] It's a raid.

you come upstairs to my humble abode, gentlemen? I've got a couple of interesting things to show you . . .'

That did it. All thought of potential deserters hiding out in this house of horror fled immediately from the minds of the two bulls. Moments later Otto heard them running down the street as if the devil himself were after them, while the Witch leaned against the wall, choking with laughter, the tears streaming down her raddled, toothless old face.

Next morning, Otto and the Count 'volunteered'.

'Dinant,' snapped Wolf, his breath fogging on the icy afternoon air, as he struck the conqueror's pose, back erect, legs wide astride, glasses focused on the scene below.

Around him, the men of the two teams stared at the long loop of the Meuse, the cluster of red-brick houses around the grey gothic cathedral that dominated the Belgian town, and the stone bridge spanning the river – at least, all of them save the Seadog, who was engaged once more with his 'grog'.

'That bridge,' Wolf lectured them, 'is vital to the success of our operation. It is one of six between here and Liège, and our objective is to capture them all so that our victorious panzers can sweep westwards as they did in 1940, and throw that Anglo-American scum back into the sea.'

Count von der Weide's face glowed at the memory – although his only part in that great victory four years before had been to run a mobile brothel for the rank-and-file.[1] Otto, for his part, was tempted to snort, 'Oh, for fart's sake, Wolf or whatever your name is, get on with it! You'd think you were old Rundstedt himself.' But instead, he merely asked, mildly enough, 'What's the drill, Wolf?'

Wolf turned to him stiffly, as if he were suffering from a sore neck. 'No time to waste, eh, Tex! Drill? I'll tell you.

[1] See *Otto's Blitzkrieg!* for further details.

As is customary in structures which have some strategic value, the bridge will be equipped with detonator chambers, which will have been filled with high explosive by the Amis.' He indicated the dark figures moving slowly back and forth across the bridge, their weapons slung over their shoulders, occasionally stopping to check the passes of the townsfolk and examine a horse-drawn cart or one of the ancient coal-driven trucks. 'Their job is to guard those explosive chambers, so that they can be detonated as soon as danger threatens. It will be our task to ensure that those explosives are *not* set off – and, more importantly, that the Amis don't *know* we have sabotaged the explosives until it is too late and our panzers come racing down this hill.'

As he spoke, Wolf's blue eyes suddenly glowed with fanatical zeal, and Otto felt a cold finger of fear trace its way the length of his spine. People like Wolf, who were prepared to die for Folk, Fatherland and Führer without a moment's hesitation, were dangerous. They could get you killed – right smartish.

'Now,' Wolf continued, while Lynx and Jaguar listened to him gleaming-eyed, 'I intend to tackle those chambers under cover of darkness and *after* curfew has been imposed. That way we won't have any of those decadent Belgie swine blocking our way down to the boats.'

'Ahoy, there, matey,' the Seadog broke in suddenly, between swigs of raw rum, 'yer can't do that, yer know!'

All of them turned and stared at the old man, who looked completely absurd in his GI uniform, his cap set at the back of his head like a grey-haired, drunken Napoleon.

'What did you say?' Wolf barked.

'I said *you can't do that*, matey.'

'Do what?' Wolf's voice was icy and full of latent menace. Behind him; Otto tensed, he could see that the SS man was liable to explode any moment.

'Take a boat into that river,' the Seadog said, unmoved.

'Why on earth not?'

'Because the current out there midstream is eight to ten

knots, matey. Yer'd need arms like a gorilla if you was thinking of getting up the bridge from the central pillar – that's why.'

Otto stared at the one-legged old man in open-mouthed amazement. It was the longest speech he had ever heard the Seadog make since the first day at the remote camp, where he had spotted him sprawled blind-drunk in the guard-room, false teeth in a glass at his side, his wooden leg detached, and a hand-printed sign around his neck that read: 'IF FOUND, PLEASE RETURN TO GRAFENWOEHR CAMP, BAVARIA!' In the interests of security the 'Grafenwoehr' had been poorly scored through and replaced by an 'X'.

'But how do you know?' Wolf said, slightly put out by this display of expert knowledge on the Seadog's part.

''Cos, I'm yer river expert,' the Seadog replied stoutly. 'Sailed every river from Rotterdam to Regensburg. Many's the time I've been thrown out of the grog-shops down there in Dinant – and other places as well, when I was younger and had my strength.' To make his meaning entirely plain, he made an obscene gesture with his thumb and two fingers and leered knowingly.

Wolf flushed crimson at such crudity. In his view sex was an unwarrantable distraction from the holy business of dying for one's Fatherland.

'So, river expert,' he snapped, 'if we can't take a boat, how do we reach those detonator chambers then?'

The Seadog took his time before replying, scratching his grizzled skull for effect and obviously enjoying being the centre of interest for a change. 'Well, matey, the Dinant bridge is one of them old 'uns, built – oh, I don't know, years ago. It's only supported by one central pillar. Now, *you* thought from looking at the photos that the only way to get to that central support was by water, didn't you? Well . . .' He paused, savouring what was to come. 'It ain't.'

'It ain't?' the Count echoed, and clicked his tongue in irritation. 'I mean, it *isn't*, er, Seadog?'

'No, it ain't. Yer see, when I used to do this route in the old days, Rotterdam-Liège-Dinant-Thionville-Metz . . .'

'Oh, for God's sake, get on with it!' Wolf snapped angrily.

'I'm getting there,' the Seadog said, quite unruffled. 'Well, in *them* days, back in the Twenties, the Belgie women didn't wear no drawers, see – at least, the poorer women didn't.'

Wolf's eyes blazed at this revelation, but he controlled himself in time. Otto, for his part, listened in open-mouthed awe. What was the silly old fool rabbiting on about?

'Now, like I was saying, the Belgies used to come onto the bridge of a morning to empty their slops into the river – yer know, their piss-buckets and the like.'

'How fascinating,' the Count breathed. 'What a sordid life the poor must lead!'

'And of course, they'd stand with their legs apart. So what could yer poor old sailorboy do? I mean, there wasn't much entertainment on the barges in them days – mostly yer five-fingered widow of an evening' – he made an explicit gesture with his right hand – 'perhaps a game of *skat*, and a grog if you was lucky.'

'For God's sake!' screamed Wolf, face crimson with exasperation.

'I'm coming to it,' the Seadog said calmly, smiling fondly as the old memories came flooding back. 'So we looked up, didn't we? It was our only entertainment on boring days. All that gash! Never seen anything like it in all me life!'

By now, Wolf was twisting his neck to one side, eyes popping out of his head, spluttering for breath, as if he were being slowly strangled. But just as he was about to erupt in fury, Seadog produced his trump card.

'*That*'s how I came to notice that there's a catwalk under the bridge.'

'*A catwalk!*' they echoed as one.

'Yeah – so that the repair crews, the painters and the like, could get underneath it to carry out their jobs. 'Spect that's how the Ami engineers got to them chambers you was talking about to plant their charges.' He slumped back in the jeep, reaching for the rum bottle, his rheumy eyes misted over, once more lost in his memories.

'Them was the days,' he breathed to himself. 'The sights you saw on that bridge in them days! Gash galore, it was!' He took a hearty swig of his grog. '*Gash galore* . . .'

Now the Seadog was forgotten. Wolf had recovered his composure, and Otto could almost see his mind racing as he absorbed the information and worked out how to put it to best use. There was a pause as he deliberated, and Lynx and Jaguar bent stiffly forward, heads and faces rigid with tension as they awaited their comrade's announcement. As for the Count, he hummed 'South of the Border' under his breath – obviously he was taking his new role of 'Mex', the Mexican corporal, extremely seriously. Otto half-expected the old ham to stick a flower behind his ear and break into a Flamenco dance.

'Right,' Wolf snapped at last, 'this is the drill. We move out as soon as it's dark. You and you,' he indicated Lynx and Jaguar, 'will cover the sentries on the eastern bank of the Meuse.'

They clicked to attention and acknowledged the order with a brisk salute.

'You and you,' he nodded to the Count and Seadog, 'will stay with the jeeps to the left of that large rock at two o'clock, down on the riverbank. If anything goes wrong you're to drive up at full speed and pick us up. Got it?'

The Seadog grunted something, obviously still taken up with his memories of 'gash galore'. The Count, on the other hand, radiated enthusiasm.

'I knew it!' he said eagerly. 'I knew! The Great Game is commencing!' He clicked his heels, adding an exuberant '*Olé*' for good measure.

Finally Wolf turned to Otto, whose heart began to sink

into his lower regions as those hard, blue eyes focused on his broad, honest working-class face.

'Tex, as you're the one who speaks this Ami slang of theirs best, you will accompany me. It'll be dangerous, I know, but I'm relying on you. After all,' he added, with a look that suggested that he knew far more than he was revealing, '*nomen es omen* – isn't that right?' And he winked slowly.

Otto groaned. There it was again: *nomen es omen*. How often he'd heard that phrase from idiots like Wolf! And every time it had landed him right up to his hooter in shit. Like a condemned man, he lowered his young head and waited for execution to be served . . .

DAY TWO: SATURDAY, DECEMBER 16th, 1944

'When you're up to yer hooter in crap – don't open yer mouth.'

The sayings of Otto Stahl

'*Now!*' hissed Wolf.

Otto took a last look up the bridge road. All was silent, save for the soft tread of the sentry's boots as he paced out the last ten metres of his beat. In another minute, he would turn and begin the return journey back. Otto breathed in hard and swung himself over the parapet. Far down below – it seemed at that moment to be a kilometre drop at least – there was the faint gleam of the River Meuse. Nerves tingling electrically with apprehension and fear, he let go.

His knees crashed against the stone. Instinctively his hands shot out. A nail ripped away, but he stifled the yelp of agony. Next instant he felt something metallic and hard. It was the catwalk. He grabbed hold of it and felt his arms nearly wrenched from their shoulder sockets.

For a long moment he just hung there, swinging back and forth, fighting to get his breath back, desperately trying to forget that he was hanging by his fingertips right above the river Meuse so far below. Next instant, Wolf came tumbling down, and with a harsh gasp grabbed hold of the metal stanchion next to him.

'*Move*,' he commanded in an urgent whisper. 'For God's sake, *move*, man – or are you going to hang there all damned night?'

Otto gulped hard. He hadn't even the strength to answer the fanatical fool. With a grunt, he started to lever himself upwards, feeling the muscles of his back suddenly blaze with pain as red-hot pincers of agony nipped at his shoulders. He got one knee on the stanchion and then the other, kneeling there as if in prayer, sobbing for breath. Next to him, Wolf hauled himself upwards effortlessly.

'Come on, follow me,' he ordered, and without waiting for Otto, he began crawling on his hands and knees along the stanchion towards the dimly-glimpsed, cage-like structure of the catwalk described by the Seadog.

Reluctantly, propelled forward by naked will-power, Otto followed.

Time passed slowly. The only sound was their own harsh breathing and the distant thunder of the water below growing louder now as they approached the centre of the bridge. Otto crawled on, keeping his eyes fixed firmly on Wolf's skinny arse, not daring to look down to where the water raced under the bridge at ten knots, its surface scummed with foam.

Suddenly Wolf stopped, and Otto nearly blundered into him.

'Watch your step, man!' Wolf hissed angrily. 'Try to look where you're going!'

'Christ, I've never concentrated so hard in my whole shitting life!' Otto blurted out furiously. '*Himmel, Arsch und Wolkenbruch*, do you think I'm going along with my eyes closed?'

'Quiet,' Wolf snapped, 'I think we've reached the chamber.'

'Yeah - it *smells* like a piss-pot all right,' Otto snarled, nostrils suddenly assailed by the ammoniac stench of stale urine. 'Half the old nags in Belgium must have taken a leak in here - and a tom-tit as well, I shouldn't wonder!'

Wolf ignored the comment. Carefully, he switched on the little blue flashlight attached to his tunic, the beam shaded above so that it shone downwards. A low cavern of stone came into view, its walls scaled with nitre, wet, dripping and evil-smelling, with a series of multi-coloured wires leading into it. Wolf raised the light a little so that the two of them crouched on the narrow wet catwalk could see deeper inside. As Wolf had predicted, there at the back were rows of white tubes, each row neatly wired to the other.

'TNT,' Wolf whispered, 'enough there to blow the bridge at Dinant to hell and back.' He reached out his right hand as if to move inside, but Otto caught him hurriedly.

'Wait a minute, you fool!' he hissed. 'The Amis aren't *that* dumb. They might have booby-trapped the place just so some idiot like you can get his turnip blown off.'

For once Wolf wasn't offended by Otto's coarse tone. Instead he said warmly, 'Of course, Tex, you're right. I can see you're a professional.'

Otto grunted something, and the two of them set about searching the entrance to the cavern for trick devices. Within a minute they had found it: a spring-release detonator looking for all the world like a metallic book of matches, held down by a small stone that would have been knocked off by anyone crawling inside unawares. A thin wire concealed in the dust of centuries, led from the detonator to the packed rows of TNT.

Wolf nodded his approval and then, pulling up the clippers attached to his belt by a chain, snipped the wire in two. Moments later they were crawling inside, and Wolf was issuing his instructions.

'Cut any and every wire you can see, Tex, while I check behind the explosive in case they had some reserve detonating system – and watch how you go. Absolutely no noise. Remember, the other sentry at the far end of the bridge can't be more than twenty metres away from us now.'

Otto nodded and in the dim, blue light cast by the blacked-out torch, he commenced his task, his hands trembling like leaves and his fingers feeling as clumsy as if they were clothed in boxing-gloves.

Meanwhile, Wolf clambered to the rear of the stone chamber, busily prodding around behind the rows of taped TNT and searching for a possible alternative system. He seemed to be quite unconcerned by the fact that if anything went wrong, both he and Otto would be blown sky-high.

Five minutes went by. Ten. Now Otto was almost finished. With a bit of luck, once it was all over and they were back on *terra firma* safely again, their mission would be finished. Hadn't that been the rumour back at Grafenwoehr? Their two teams were scheduled to immobilize the bridge at Dinant – and that was all. Soon they'd be back in the Reich, and he and that romantic fool of a Count could both take an immediate dive. The 'Great Game' would be over for ever. Then they could sit out the rest of the war in some remote provincial town, waiting for the Amis to arrive and end this mess for good.

With a groan he struggled to his feet and wiped away the sweat which had formed on his brow.

'All right, Wolf?' he queried softly. 'I'm about done now.'

Suddenly Wolf froze.

A thin beam of white light had swept down from above, swinging back and forth and casting their grotesquely magnified shadows on the wall of the chamber. Both remained motionless, their hearts beating furiously, nerves jingling electrically.

'Hey, is anybody down there?' called a soft, uncertain American voice.

Wolf shot Otto a look of alarm. It was the sentry all right. He raised his finger to his suddenly pale lips. Otto nodded his understanding; he couldn't have spoken, even if he'd wanted to.

'Hey, you down there!' The American voice was harder now. 'I know you're down there . . . Now sound off, guy, or there'll be trouble!'

Wolf acted. 'Talk,' he whispered. 'Keep him talking, Tex.' Next instant he had wriggled noiselessly out of the chamber, leaving Otto squatting there hopelessly. What the hell did you say to an American sentry in the middle of the night, sitting on a bridge thirty metres above the Meuse?

'Hello,' he said tentatively.

'Hello, my aching ass!' the American snapped angrily. 'What in Sam Hill are ya doing there?'

'I . . . er . . . lost something!' Otto ventured helplessly.

'Lost something?'

'Yeah. I was walking over the bridge and it . . . er . . . it dropped out of my pocket and rolled down under the bridge . . . It was a silver dollar,' he added hurriedly, in what he thought was a flash of genius.

Up above him, the unknown American gasped audibly. '*A silver dollar!* Are you nuts? Risking your neck for a lousy buck! Buddy, you must be ready for a Section Eight.'

Otto hadn't the faintest idea what a 'Section Eight' was, but he seized on the phrase gratefully. 'No, I don't think I'd like that.'

'What the fuck d'ya mean, you wouldn't like it?' the sentry cried in exasperation. Otto heard a sudden metallic click as the American drew back the bolt of his rifle. 'Now, come on up out of there, buddy, with your mitts in the air.'

'But how can I get up there with – '

'Out, brother, *out!*'

Miserably Otto crawled out of the chamber with the beam of light now aimed directly into his eyes and nearly blinding him.

'Please,' he said, 'I can't see – you're dazzling me.'

'Okay, but no funny business, or you're gonna be deader than King Kong's dong. Move it brother!'

Otto 'moved it'. As best he could, he climbed up the parapet, while the sentry backed off, Garand tucked to one hip, torch following Otto's every movement as he swung his leg over the stanchion.

'Now just hold it there, buddy,' the sentry commanded, seeing for the first time that Otto was dressed in American Army uniform. 'Okay, now let's see some ID, *toot-sweet!*'

Otto made a pretence of fumbling with the upper pocket of his Ike jacket. Behind the sentry, a dark figure detached itself from the shadows. It was Wolf, advancing on the unsuspecting American, ready for the kill. Otto wanted to cry out, stop him, *do* something; but he knew helplessly there was nothing he could do to prevent what was going to happen next. The sentry *had* to die! Desperately he continued to fumble with the button of his pocket, as if it were stiff and he couldn't open it.

'Hurry it up, buddy. It's colder than a witch's tit out –'

The words ended in a soft moan, as Wolf's hand clamped round the sentry's mouth. In the very same instant he slid the killing blade between the third and fourth rib – savagely hard. The American's knees buckled immediately. But Wolf was taking no chances: his knife thrust home again – and again. The rifle clattered to the cobbles and Otto jumped, his heart beating like a frantic trip-hammer.

'Quick!' Wolf hissed, still holding onto the American. 'He's dead . . . Give me a hand.'

On legs of rubber, Otto somehow or other staggered over to where Wolf held the dead American, whose helmet had slipped grotesquely over his face. Killer and victim looked like lovers clasped in a fervent embrace.

'What you gonna do with him?' Otto croaked.

Wolf flashed a look to left and right. The sentry at the far end of the bridge was nowhere to be seen. 'Get rid of him.'

'But you said nobody should know we've cut the wires –'

'They won't,' Wolf hissed. 'They'll think he's done a bunk at first. The Amis are always wandering off and getting lost. By the time his dead body's washed up, it'll be too late – the bridge will be in German hands. Here, give me a hand.' He grunted, and with Otto's help, thrust the body over the parapet. There was a soft splash as it plunged into the Meuse. Next moment, the murdered man's rifle and helmet followed, and the two of them were clambering back the way they had come.

Ten minutes later, just as the big clock in the centre of

the riverside town chimed the first hour of the new day, Wolf flashed a glance at his watch and said, 'Well, gentlemen, this is a holy day – the first day of the great new offensive which will sweep that rabble back into the sea. In exactly four and a half hours, the great drive westwards will commence.'

'And now that we've done *our* bit,' Otto said hopefully, as the four of them hurried to the waiting jeeps through the sleeping, blacked-out town, 'I suppose we can go home, eh?'

Jaguar sniggered, and Lynx muttered something under his breath to Wolf, who sniggered too.

'Or do we lie low here until our troops reach Dinant?' Otto asked. 'I expect they'll want us to stick around until they've captured the bridge or something eh, Wolf?'

But Wolf remained obstinately, ominously silent.

Otto was suddenly overcome by a sinking awareness that there was more to this undercover mission of theirs than mere sabotaging of the detonator chambers on the bridge. Miserably, he trailed after them until the night had swallowed them up, and all was silent again, save for the distant sound of the Meuse . . .

It had been dead of night when they had finally descended at Grafenwoehr Station – a weary, unshaven bunch of 'volunteers', stiff after the long journey and a little bewildered by the blazing arc lights.

They were from all branches of the services: Air Force, SS, Army, Navy, Merchant Marine, most in their mid-twenties and many of them highly-decorated veterans. Looking around at the faces of the others, Otto dug his elbow in the Count's ribs.

'Just cast your glassy orbs on this bunch! Do *they* look the type to be doing some sort of rear-échelon stallion type of job? *Eh?*'

The Count did as he was ordered and nodded his head

reluctantly. 'Perhaps you're right, my dear boy. They do look rather a hardy collection of individuals.'

'*Hardy*, my arse, Count!' Otto said crudely. 'These fellers are the survivors. They've been around. They know the score – and then some.'

'Don't worry, Otto,' the Count soothed, 'everything will turn out all right on the day.'

'*Achtung!*'

A harsh, metallic voice suddenly boomed out from the loudspeaker directly above their heads, echoing and re-echoing through the station hall – a gloomy building whose sole decoration was the slogan of that year of defeat. WHEELS ROLL FOR VICTORY.

'*Alle herhören!*'

Dutifully they listened. 'From this moment you do not exist. You are non-persons. Is that understood? Any attempt to make contact with the outside world will result in the most severe penalties. *Klar?*'

Like the rough, tough, experienced soldiers they all were, the 'volunteers' looked unimpressed. One of them attempted an insolent, contemptuous fart, but without effect. There was something very frightening about the detached, forceful voice in that remote, lonely station, with the arc lights blazing down from above.

'In one minute the trucks will arrive to take you to your new home,' the harsh metallic voice boomed on. 'You will make no attempt to converse with the men in those trucks, and even if you did, it would be completely useless, for none of them speaks a word of German. *Klar?* Prepare to move out.'

The veterans looked at each other, attempting to feign indifference, but the worried look in their eyes told a different story. All of them, experienced as they were, were unnerved by this strange place and even stranger treatment. What in Heaven's name had they let themselves in for?

The next few days had increased their bewilderment

even more. Grafenwoehr Camp was completely sealed off from the outside world, guarded by squat little men who wore the uniform of the Waffen SS, but spoke no German and conversed with each other in what appeared to be some sort of Asiatic tongue. But then, even the 'volunteers' themselves were under strict orders not to speak German during duty hours. From now onwards the language of the camp was English – or as their instructors – mostly university professors, who seemed oddly out of place in their too-tight US summer uniforms – called it contemptuously, 'US slang'.

As November, 1944, gave way to December, their training for whatever mission the High Command had in store for them intensified. They learned how to relax 'American-style' and spent mornings on the barracks square just lounging around, propping up walls or sitting on their haunches, while their portly, bespectacled instructor pleaded with them to 'relax, gentlemen, *relax!*'

They learned how to chew gum. 'For Chrissake, guys,' their instructor cursed at his unhappy squad each of whom was equipped with a stick of captured US gum, 'it ain't goddam poison! Chew the goddam stuff as if you was enjoying it. Now, on the command three, let's see you chewing and smiling! One . . . Two . . . Three . . . *Chew!*'

They even learned how to walk American-style, under the supervision of an earnest professor of sociology who claimed to have made a 'serious study' of the subject. It was the professor's contention that the US walk was 'a deliberate cultivated, male-ego-boosting, provoking manner of gait, probably influenced by the lack of female consorts at the frontier in the 19th century.' As Otto commented in disgust, after being told for the second time to roll his hips, 'Christ, Count, I feel like a warm brother trying to sell his arse in the *Unter den Linden*!'

In that first week of December, lessons in American dancing and singing were introduced too, and the camp shook to the brassy rhythms of Harry James and the

Andrew Sisters as they belted out the 'Boogie-Woogie Bugle Boy of Company B'. Now earnest SS officers and burly paratroopers made their first clumsy attempts at 'jiving', urged on by the professor, with 'Vat is kooking, Yackson?' and 'Zee you later, alligator!' As Otto moaned after the Count had stepped on his toe for the second time, 'God in heaven, if the Führer only knew what was going on right under his nose!'

'But it's fun, don't you think, Otto?' the Count replied with a beam. 'So delightfully New World and uninhibited – totally different from the waltz.' Just then the music switched to Glenn Miller's 'In the Mood', and before Otto could catch his breath, the two of them were whirling around and gyrating frenziedly, surrounded by a red-faced, embarrassed mob of similarly cavorting soldiers.

Naturally the rumours about their mission flew thick and fast, especially after the first consignment of captured US tanks and jeeps reached them in their remote hide-out. Each night as they squatted side by side in the eight-man 'crappers', they passed the latest news from one to another in hushed whispers, their gaze fixed on the doors in case they were overheard. 'They say we're gonna land on the French coast and break into German-held Lorient . . .' 'We're to be used to paradrop on our POWs held by the Amis in France. We'll release them and start a revolt behind enemy lines . . .' 'We're going to re-capture Aachen the same way the Amis did, by wearing the other side's uniforms . . .'

Otto's apprehension increased daily, and even the Count now admitted that he had made a '*miscalculation*', as he called it.

'*Miscalculation!*' Otto echoed angrily. 'You've gone and landed us right in the shit, that's what you've done with your sodding Great Game!'

'But it *is* an adventure, isn't it?' the Count protested mildly. 'I mean, it *does* relieve the monotony of our drab old lives.'

'Should I put that on your tombstone, Count?' Otto sneered.

On December 8th, Otto and the Count were introduced to the members of the 'Zoo' and to Seadog, who as always was already half-drunk and insisted on singing 'A Life on the Ocean Waves', all the way to Moosberg POW camp. Here they spent two days mingling with the 20,000 American prisoners held there, in order to give their crash course in things American 'the final polish', as their instructor in 'relaxing' optimistically called it. All that Otto learned was that Americans played a mean game of poker, and that lice in Moosberg came 'king-sized' – like everything else in the land of Uncle Sam.

Wolf, who was obviously destined to be their leader in whatever was to come, was not impressed either. As soon as they were out of the camp and on their way back to Grafenwoehr, he ripped off the dirty American jeep coat that he had been wearing and sneered: 'What a bunch, eh! The products of Democracy and the Great New World! Dirty, unshaven undisciplined, the lot of them. Not a soldier among them. Degenerates, the whole pack!'

'They make good bootleg booze, though,' the Seadog commented, as he unstrapped his leg and settled back in the truck.

'Yes,' the Count agreed, 'I thought they were quite kind. That big black chap in my hut kept suggesting that I should go to the latrines with him after lights out because he had a little treat for me. Pity I didn't have the time. Wonder what it was? I know it was something he kept in his pocket, because he was always feeling – '

'Oh shut up, Count!' Otto snapped, scratching miserably. Otto couldn't share his companion's blithe optimism; he knew instinctively as he watched Wolf's hard, harsh face that the former SS officer meant trouble for Frau Stahl's handsome son – a lot of trouble. And soon . . .

Two days after their return to Grafenwoehr, the whole camp was paraded for a speech from Otto Skorzeny, who towered head and shoulders above his SS adjutants as he swaggered to the rostrum, a faint, knowing smile on his sabre-slashed face.

'*Morgan, Soldaten!*' he cried to the ranks of men below.

'*Morgan Obersturmbannführer!*' they answered in hoarse unison, their breath fogging grey on the keen morning air.

'God in Heaven,' Skorzeny said, staring down at them with a faint grin on his sallow face. 'You're standing there like Prussian guardsmen! Fine bunch of Amis *you* make. *Relax* – and that's an order!'

They 'relaxed', and a few of them grinned happily. Otto's face, however, remained sourly sombre, and apprehensive. He knew Skorzeny's kind, they always sent men to their deaths with a few cheery words, a joke or two and a bit of patriotic pep-talk. It was something they were taught in their leadership courses at the war academy; it was all part of the big, fake front that professional officers presented to the world. Otto wasn't impressed. He'd seen it all before, and each time it had spelled one thing: danger.

'Soldiers, you are the élite of the élite. All of the three thousand men of my new 150th Panzer Brigade are skilled soldiers, trained in battle. But you are more. You are not only battle-experienced veterans –'

Next to Otto, the Count thrust out his chest proudly, jutting his jaw and doing his best to look every inch the seasoned professional fighting man. Inwardly Otto groaned. The Count was slipping into a new role yet again. Now he was the hard-bitten veteran. This was his 'war face', class one.

'– But also,' continued Skorzeny, 'skilled linguists. Every one of you is a perfect American-speaker. It is for that reason that I have picked this section of my Brigade for *special tasks*.'

Otto waited, eyes narrowed to slits, his mind racing furiously. *What special tasks?* Already he was wondering if he could get out of what was to come before it was too late.

'Shortly,' Skorzeny continued in that easy Viennese

manner of his, 'you will be divided up into what are called jeep-teams – three men to a jeep. These teams will infiltrate the Ami front – and prepare the way for *our great new counter-offensive in the West!*'

At this point, an excited, jubilant murmuring broke out among Skorzeny's listeners. Someone said fervently, 'What an honour!' Another exclaimed, 'This is a cause worth dying for!' And at Otto's side, the Count proclaimed proudly, 'Germany will triumph again . . . *We march once more!*'

But Otto's heart sank into his boots. It was what he had feared all along. The hated National Socialist cause, which he had sworn back in '39 *never* to fight for, had him by the short and curlies yet again. And it was all the Count's fault! At that moment, he could have happily castrated the old buffoon with a blunt razorblade.

Skorzeny held up his hands for silence. 'I thought the news would startle you, comrades! Who would have thought three months ago that our beloved Fatherland would ever march into battle again? But now, our task. Our divisions will drive westwards through the Ardennes; but before they do so, it will be the objective of this Brigade to secure the bridges across the River Meuse, spread alarm and confusion among the Amis, and generally sabotage their communications so that we can facilitate the Wehrmacht's push towards Antwerp and Brussels.' He paused and let his words sink in, a hesitant look on his scarred face, as if he were considering just how he should formulate his next words. 'There are, too, certain . . . special tasks reserved for some of you. Naturally I shall brief you individually on those missions. But before I do, let me say just this. Comrades, soon some of you will be entering enemy territory, wearing enemy uniform. If you are captured, you will be treated as a spy – and I do not need to remind you of the penalty for spying . . .'

Dead right you don't! thought Otto with a shudder.

They lean you against the backyard wall and blast a shitting great hole in you – that's what they do to spies!

'I know, comrades, that you are all brave men, tried and tested time and time again on the battlefield . . .'

The Count's jaw jutted even more. Otto could hear him grinding his teeth mercilessly as he once more put on his 'veteran' look.

' . . . But even brave men have been known to weaken under torture and betray their comrades. Thus, I decree that each one of you will know only enough of what is planned to be able to carry out his own mission successfully. Thus, no offer of freedom from execution made by a perfidious enemy will be able to induce any man to betray the mission of his comrades. Soldiers of the 150th Panzer Brigade, I salute you!' Skorzeny's right arm suddenly shot out rigidly, and at the top of his voice be bellowed, '*Sieg Heil!*'

'*Sieg Heil!*' the volunteers barked back fervently, eyes sparkling fanatically – all save Otto Stahl, who knew it wouldn't be long now before the balloon went up, carrying him and the Count on what might well be an Ascension Day mission.[1]

Two hours later Skorzeny left, but not before conferring earnestly with the 'Zoo', to whose jeep-teams, Otto, the Count, and the drunken old sailor Seadog had been assigned. With ever-growing alarm, Otto noted that Skorzeny had some sort of film run for the Zoo's benefit. He could see the flickering lights coming from the camp office, and a couple of times while he idled outside, he could hear snatches of sound in English. At one point he could just make out the words 'But my dear General . . .', spoken by a rumbling, throaty voice that seemed vaguely familiar. It was all very strange and alarming.

But if Otto was alarmed, the Count was beside himself with excitement. As they reported for the afternoon American dancing session and the first strains of Bing

[1] *i.e.* a one-way mission.

Crosby's latest hit 'White Christmas' wafted over the loudspeaker, he stretched out his arms to his surly-faced comrade, crying joyfully, 'Come, Otto, my boy, let's enjoy this one! It'll probably be the last time we'll dance together before the day of victory.'

Thus the two old running-mates, one grim and silent, the other gay and excited, danced their way to victory, to the accompaniment of the Old Groaner himself.

It was the faint, ominous rumble to the east which woke Otto. For a few minutes he lay in the comforting warmth of his sleeping bag, staring at the cold, silver stars studding the hard black sky, unable to grasp what the sound was. Then he realized: it was gunfire – a lot of it. The great counter-offensive had started! Suddenly he felt happier than he had in days. Soon the Wehrmacht's leading units would smash their way through the enemy lines – for the Amis were very thin on the ground in this part of the front – and their mission would be over. Perhaps a cynical little voice at the back of his mind *did* warn him things might not work out *quite* like that. But Otto ignored it. Instead, he crawled out of his sleeping bag, shivering as the cold struck him and urinated in a stream of hissing, steaming yellow. He was just thinking about looking for something to eat, when he heard the faint metallic crackle of their long-range radio.

He turned, startled. For a moment he couldn't work out quite where the sound was coming from; then he had it. Someone was crouched in the low roof of the ruined cottage where they had hidden the jeeps, obviously taking advantage of the height in order to transmit. Otto crept forward curiously, cocking his head to the faint breeze so as to hear better. As he had half-expected it was Wolf – the former SS officer never seemed to sleep. This time, it looked as if he was receiving some sort of orders from whoever it was he was speaking to. '*Jawohl . . . Jawohl . . .*' he kept repeating, in that stiff, wooden fashion of his. '*Es wird gemacht.*'

Once, however, Otto did catch something other than that stupid '*Jawohl*'. It was a name – and Wolf was repeating it, as if he wasn't completely sure that he'd heard it correctly.

'Diedenhofen, you said?' he queried. '. . . *Jawohl, Diedenhofen.*'

It was only five minutes after Wolf had finished speaking and was beginning to pack away the aerial that Otto remembered where he'd heard the name before: it was the old German name for the French border city of Thionville, which lay somewhere to their south. He frowned in the darkness, while around him the little camp slowly began to come to life. But what in three devils' name was so important about Diedenhofen-alias-Thionville?

Six hours later, Wolf told them.

All morning they had been heading south, fighting the traffic streaming to the front and away from it: great straggling lines of peasants with their possessions piled high on ancient farm-carts, coaches, wheelbarrows – all fleeing westwards, with here and there an American truck, struggling through the tide of refugees, filled with frightened GIs who invariably greeted them with cries of, 'It's the big bug-out, guys! The Krauts are coming – millions of 'em!'

Now they had pulled off the road and into an abandoned quarry, heating their C-ration spam over the burning cardboard boxes in which the rations came and gratefully sipping their instant coffee, while the guns rumbled steadily at the front and the refugees streamed by. It was as if the whole of Eastern Belgium was heading west.

'Everyone listen to me,' Wolf announced suddenly.

Otto shot a quick look at the other two members of the Zoo. They were smiling stiffly to themselves, letting the warm steam from the canteens wreathe about their hard faces. It looked to Otto very much as if they already knew what Wolf had to say and were pleased with that knowledge.

The Count put down the GI spade on which he was frying the spam. The Seadog lowered his bottle. By now it was clear to all of them that they wouldn't be returning to the Reich. Obviously Wolf had something else in store for them, and they were eager to know what it was.

Wolf took his time, obviously savouring the surprise he was about to spring upon them.

'Of course, you must be wondering why we're heading south to France when our great counter-offensive is being launched through Belgium, here. You must also have realized, even you, Seadog' – and he shot a sour look at the old sailor, who was firmly clutching his grog as if he was terrified that someone might take it away from him – 'that the sabotaging of the bridge at Dinant was only *part* of our mission.'

There was a pause as he let his words sink in, and the Count, whose spam was now turning black unnoticed, exclaimed excitedly, 'I say, Wolf, how thrilling! Tell us more, please.'

Wolf gave him a cold look. 'You remember what Obersturmbannführer Skorzeny said, Mex, about the need to know? One always has to be on one's guard against traitors.'

'Traitors!' Seadog sneered. 'Not among us, surely, matey?'

Wolf looked disapprovingly at the bottle the old sailor was clutching, but made no further comment. Instead he went on, 'We've been ordered to head for Diedenhofen and to cross the frontier with the refugees. I've been told it's guarded by French civilian police, so they'll present no danger to us Americans. Once we're in Diedenhofen, we shall receive further instructions from a sleeper-agent planted by Skorzeny back in September, when the Wehrmacht was forced to withdraw from France. With effect from this morning, Skorzeny has re-activated him.'

'Oh, for God's sake,' Otto cried in exasperation, 'get on with it, Wolf! What kind of instructions is this idiot of a sleeper-agent going to give us, eh?'

Wolf's harsh, vulpine face broke into a tight smile. 'That I do not know, Tex,' he said slowly, savouring his words, while the other two SS men leaned forward in anticipation, the same cold little smile on their thin, cruel lips. 'But this I *do* know. It will be connected with our new assignment.' He hesitated, the two other members of the Zoo nodded encouragingly, willing him to continue. Wolf's voice sank to a whisper and he stared dramatically around the faces of his listeners. 'Gentlemen we are going to kill someone – someone *very* important . . .'

DAY THREE: SUNDAY, DECEMBER 17th 1944

'The trip was further complicated by the extraordinary fears entertained by the Security Corps that enemy murderers were circulating in the area with the hope of killing Montgomery, Bradley, and me, and possibly others.'

General Eisenhower, 1944

It was a perfect late December afternoon. Outside the tall windows of the 18th century chateau, soft flakes of snow were drifting down silently. Inside, however, it was snug and warm, with the logs crackling merrily in the grate. Next to it, Telex, Ike's black scottie, snored happily, as if he, too, like most of the staff officers at Supreme Headquarters, was sleeping off the hangover after the party the Boss had given the night before. As for the Boss himself, he dozed on the elegant French couch, wearing the slippers that Mamie had given him, an unread Western clutched to his chest, a half-consumed whisky highball on the carpet beside him.

The tall, slender red-head in the uniform of the American Army smiled warmly at the sleeping General. How he loved those Westerns! She stretched her body in a svelte manner befitting a former fashion model, and looked at the ormolu clock on the marble mantelpiece. It was nearly half-past three. In five minutes she would ring for tea. She knew the General hated it, but she insisted that tea-time meant precisely what it said. Then she would toast the crumpets. Unfortunately, she and the General had run out of strawberry jam and unsalted butter, but no doubt in due course some visitor or other would supply the missing items. The General only had to mention he fancied this or that foodstuff and he would be swamped with gifts. Once he had happened to remark that he liked oysters, and the whole place had smelled like Billingsgate for days afterwards. She had taken him severely to task over that, forbidding him to go to the front for three days as a punishment for his lack of consideration. Still, he was a dear in a helpless, unromantic Mid-Western sort of way – and naturally important. Very, very important.

Her mind made up, she rang the bell to summon one of the soldier servants, and reached for the toasting fork. But Lieutenant Kay Summersby, officially the Supreme Commander's 'chaffeuse', was not fated to serve tea and crumpets that particular afternoon. For just then she heard a faint cry of 'Turn out the guard' filtering through the heavy glass of the big window. She cursed under her breath. It must be a visitor – and just when she was about to prepare tea! These days the war seemed to allow her and the General no privacy at all. Reluctantly she strode to the window in her somewhat masculine manner, and peered out into the snow.

Down below, General Strong of Intelligence was fuming. The white-helmeted US military policeman was making a great show of examining his pass, while civilians seemed to be walking in and out of the chateau gates all the time at perfect liberty. In the end the blunt Scot could contain himself no longer. 'And who the devil are those civvies, Corporal, passing through just like that?'

The MP gave him a quick grin, 'Ah well, sir, you see, I don't know them, sir. They ain't got no passes. But I *do* know you, sir.' He clicked to attention. 'Pass, friend.'

General Strong groaned.

As Strong entered the General's room, it was to see Ike attempting to struggle into his shoes, hurriedly smoothing down what was left of his hair with his other hand.

'I was just about to serve the General his crumpet, sir,' said Kay Summersby in explanation.

'So, I see, Lieutenant,' Strong answered, and blushed fiercely when he realized what he had said.

'We always have crumpet in the afternoon, Ken,' said Ike, 'Just the two of us here on the rug, in front of the fire. I find it very relaxing. Mamie and I never had crumpet.' And so saying, he flashed the Scot that ear-to-ear grin that was now famous to cinema audiences throughout the western world. 'Crumpet's great!'

'*Muffins*, sir. Perhaps you ought to say muffins! The word you use has an unfortunate connotation in English-English, if I may be permitted to say so.'

General Eisenhower looked puzzled, but he had long gotten used to doing as the English said; they seemed to have many ways that seemed strange and unfamiliar to Mid-Western boys like himself. 'Okay, Ken, if you say so – muffins it is. But where's the fire? Something wrong at the front?'

The big, dark-haired Intelligence man nodded apologetically. 'I know it's Sunday and all that, sir, but I had to see you.'

Kay Summersby frowned. Couldn't the people at the front show a little consideration? Sunday was the only day off they got. The rest of the time, she and the General didn't have a minute to call their own.

'It's definitely a large-scale counter-attack, sir,' Strong continued. 'So far we've identified nineteen German divisions belonging to two armoured armies and one infantry.'

Eisenhower whistled softly. '*Sonavabitch*!'

Once more, Kay Summersby frowned. She disliked Ike's profanity, but the habits of a lifetime in the services were hard to break. She wondered why Mamie hadn't started on her husband earlier; it would have made her task considerably easier.

'More details?' Eisenhower snapped.

'It's very difficult. The situation is terribly confused. All we know is that they're heading for the Meuse on a sixty-mile-long front between Monschau in Germany and Echternach in Luxembourg.'

'They're trying to split my First and Ninth Armies under Bradley's overall command from his Third under Patton,' Eisenhower said slowly.

'That appears to be so, sir,' Strong agreed. 'But of course, that's only one of their objectives.'

'Yes, I suppose you're right, Ken – especially seeing that they're attacking in such strength. But what are the other aims? The line of the Meuse?'

'Hard to say at the moment, sir. As I've said already, the situation up there is terribly confused, and it isn't helped by the fact that they've made a massive attempt at deception.'

'Deception?'

'Yes, sir.' Strong tapped his briefcase, which was chained to his right wrist. 'I'll let you read these documents at your leisure later, sir, after your – er . . .' he lowered his eyes discreetly '. . . muffins. They detail the enemy's attempts to fool us. In the First Army area they appear to have dropped one hundred and fifty paratroopers. Those we have captured were wearing US uniforms and carrying American identity discs – er, dog-tags. Three of them actually penetrated the main US supply dump at Stavelot.'

Once more Eisenhower whistled softly. 'Jeez, Ken those Krauts sure are cunning bastards. Excuse my French, Kay.'

Kay Summersby gave him a tight little smile, but made a mental note to give him a severe talking-to once Strong had gone and their normal Sunday activities could be resumed.

'But that's not the worst of it, sir,' Strong said grimly, tapping his case again. 'In here is a report from a German officer captured in Liège. He reveals that there's a German killer squad at large, driving US vehicles and wearing US uniforms. They're apparently escorting some *prisoners* to the rear. According to the captured German officer, these are trained SS men and completely ruthless, prepared to sell their lives in order to achieve their objective.'

'But what target are these Kraut goon squads after, Ken?'

Strong hesitated. He knew that the Supreme Commander had never before held a command in battle, never even heard a shot fired in anger. You had to treat people like that carefully. The last thing he wanted was to give the Supreme Commander a heart attack. Imagine the scandal! Everyone would put it down to the demands made on the General by his voracious red-head mistress! My God, they'd all end up on the front page of the *News of the World*!

'Well, sir,' he said slowly, 'it could be . . . you.'

To Strong's surprise, Eisenhower took it lightly. '*Me*, Ken!' he laughed. 'It's a flattering thought, but I'm too far behind the front here.' He squeezed Kay's hand reassuringly, for she had suddenly turned pale. 'No, not me.' His pale face grew grim again. 'But it could be one of the other guys – Bradley, say, or Hodges of the First. Perhaps even Patton. Yeah, now Georgie could well be their target. The Krauts sure do hate his guts.'

General Strong wasn't completely convinced, but what Eisenhower had just said did make sense. 'I take your point, sir. They're much closer to the front than you are.'

'Sure they are, Ken,' Ike said confidently. 'Hell – how could a goon squad manage to cover two or three hundred miles of the COMZ C.[1] packed with a million or more GIs? No,' he shook his head firmly, 'they ain't got a chance in hell of pulling it off.'

'Right, sir,' Strong said, rising to his feet. 'I'll contact the appropriate officers in command of security at the HQs of all field commanders and order them to take appropriate measures to protect their masters.'

'Yeah, do that,' Ike said hurriedly. His feet were hurting like hell again; he was dying to pop into his old slippers.

Strong fumbled with his left hand in his tunic pocket. 'I'll leave you the documents, sir.'

'Yes, do that, Ken. I'll read 'em up tonight. I've nearly finished *Shoot-out in the High Sierra*. Damn fine story, Ken. I can recommend it. It's about this cowpoke who's framed by the local beef baron, and – hey, what's up, Ken?'

A red-faced General Strong looked up, embarrassment

[1] The US Army's rear-area command

written all over his dark features. 'I'm afraid I've mislaid the key to the case, sir.' He swallowed hard. 'I can't get it off the damn chain.'

'Oh,' Eisenhower said, 'but I sure did want to read up on these Nazi goon squads . . .' He looked at Kay pleadingly. 'Do you think we could invite General Strong to stay with us for the crumpet – er, *muffins*, Kay, while I read 'em?'

'I – well, yes, I suppose so . . .' the red-head answered through gritted teeth. It looked like it was going to be another wasted Sunday.

'I say, sir,' General Strong said jovially, relieved that Eisenhower wasn't going to take him to task for his oversight, 'that's very sporting of you, sir, sacrificing your muffins like that. Now, I'll just switch off the self-exploding device and let you see the first document, sir.'

Thus the three of them sat in front of the crackling log fire, drinking their tea and licking the running butter off their fingers like an ageing *ménage à trois* in the deepening winter gloom, while outside the world fell to pieces . . .

Half an hour earlier, a slovenly French border guard with a World War One vintage rifle slung over his shoulder, Caporal glued to his bottom lip, shuffled up to the leading jeep and asked in a bored manner, 'Got papers, GIs?'

Wolf sneered and tossed him a pack of Chesterfield. '*Ça va*?'

'*Ça va, m'sieu*,' the soldier had agreed, catching the pack neatly. '*Passez*.' And that had been that.

Now the two jeeps were trundling slowly into the dingy border city in the gathering dusk, the grey horizon flecked here and there by the cherry-red flames of the town's blast-furnaces.

Wolf was in a nostalgic mood. 'Back in '40 I was here with the Bodyguard when we marched in. God, those were the days!' His eyes glittered with fanatical zeal at the memory. 'The Frogs thought we were creatures from another planet! A thousand of us, Germany's élite, blond and tall, not a man of us under one metre eighty-six. How the band played! How we marched that day!'

Otto watched Wolf's face, transformed suddenly, animated by emotions that he, Otto, never guessed that the SS killer possessed. Then the SS had come in as conquerors; now they were sneaking in under cover of darkness like common murderers. Times had changed. That gigantic, vulgar, black-shirted dream had been shattered. The vaunted Thousand-Year Reich of Adolf Hitler was virtually crushed – yet still these SS men refused to admit defeat. They would fight on to the bitter end. For a moment, Otto felt a sense of admiration for these bitter, hard-faced young men. They wouldn't survive the war like him and the Count, but would go down with the ship, while the rats abandoned it.

'Turn left here,' Wolf ordered. 'Our man's waiting for us in the eastern half of the dump – the German-speaking part.'

Obediently Otto turned into the dingy street leading eastwards and towards the frontier with the Reich, only fifteen-odd kilometres away. Behind him, Seadog, Jaguar and Lynx followed in the second jeep.

Both sides of the street were lined with shabby 18th century buildings, many of them pocked and scarred by the shell-fire of the battle fought here the previous September and looking as if they suffered from some loathsome skin disease. Here and there, frizzy-haired women in short art-silk dresses leaned out of the windows despite the cold, smoking silently and eyeing the passing jeeps with a knowing look.

'There seem to be a lot of females hanging about,' the Count commented innocently.

'Whores,' Otto sneered. 'For Chrissake, Count, do grow up!'

'We're now in the red-light district for the French and

the Amis,' the SS officer explained. 'An ideal cover for our man: floating population, many of them criminals . . . Nobody's going to be asking too many questions around here.' He tapped Otto on the shoulder again. 'Stop over there.'

Dutifully Otto did so. Looking around at some of the shifty types on the streets, he reckoned that if they didn't want to lose the jeep, he'd better immobilize it. Opening the hood, he took out the distributor head. Behind him, Jaguar did the same.

Seadog reeled up to Otto and Wolf, chortling happily, knowing that soon he would be able to replenish his dwindling supply of grog. 'Ahoy, Otto, you've done right, lad. But how are you going to stop 'em nicking yer tyres, eh?' And he gave a burst of drunken laughter.

'Cut that out,' Wolf commanded sharply, brushing aside a little man in a cap and carpet slippers who was trying to show him a collection of photographs of two fat women doing something highly unlikely to one another. 'Now listen. This is the drill. We split up now. Jaguar, Lynx and myself. Then you three. Six of us all together would be too conspicuous. We rendezvous at the Café de la Paix, down that street to the right and round the corner. We go first, you three next. Don't sit at the same table as we do in the café, watch out for trouble, and keep us covered. Clear?'

The three of them nodded. Wolf, who could never do anything without observing strict military precision, glanced at his watch. 'It's now exactly sixteen hundred hours. We're off. You follow in exactly five minutes at precisely sixteen hundred and five.'

'We can sodding well count, thank you!' Otto snarled.

The Count beamed happily. 'It's an adventure – a real adventure!'

Seadog's only comment was: 'Wonder where we can get a spot of grog, mates . . .'

Swiftly the first group disappeared into the milling crowds of soldiers, civilians, black-marketeers and whores that thronged the dirty cobbled street. Then, when the five minutes were up, Otto's group did the same, forcing their way through the mêlée, the Seadog hobbling along, sniffing the air for a tell-tale whiff of his precious grog.

'*Exhibition! Exhibition!*' Hissed a peddlar, sidling up to them. 'You like to see lady with donkey?'

'Don't be had,' warned the old, one-legged sailor. 'I've seen it all, from Port Said to Singapore. They kid you it's a donkey and a wench behind a screen, but it's only a couple of women.'

The Count stared open-mouthed at the eager whores, the drunken soldiers, the seedy street-vendors. 'My God, Otto,' he breathed, 'what vitality, what life! The working-class certainly knows how to live!'

Otto grinned, wondering how anyone so old could possibly be taken in by it all. They passed a Frenchman chewing razor-blades, cap on the cobbles in front of him, next to a couple of broken bottles. He was already spitting blood. A girl sitting in a doorway looked up and seeing Otto, smiled. Her lips were scarlet, her face ashen with powder, but in that flash of recognition of one lost soul for another, the girl revealed the sadness of human needs. They pushed on

'Like jig-jig, soldier?' yet another whore importuned them. 'Twenty franc, one jump . . . Fifty franc, all night.' She pouted her lips would-be seductively. 'I kiss.'

'Kiss what?' the Count asked in bewilderment. 'What does she kiss?'

'My arse,' grunted Seadog, and pushed her away. 'Lucky if you didn't catch leprosy from her kind.'

They swung round the corner and into the café, which was packed with noisy, drunken soldiers, French and American, and screaming brassy whores dressed in black silk, with dyed-blonde hair. The Count eased himself through the throng to the dripping zinc bar, littered with soggy cigarette ends.

'*Vin blanc ordinaire*,' he ordered in his fluent French.

The hard-faced barmaid gazed at him contemptuously. She sported a black eye partially hidden by a layer of thick white powder, and her cheeks were adorned with two great patches of scarlet rouge; she looked as if she were in the final stages of consumption.

'We speak GI here, brother. Nix Frog. And there ain't no wine.'

And without even waiting for the Count to change his order, she turned the tap and began to fill three dirty glasses with thin, fizzy beer.

Otto grinned and glanced at the big, fly-blown mirror behind her, his eyes narrowed against the thick clouds of blue cigarette smoke. There was Wolf. Behind him, the other two SS men sat slumped in the Grafenwoehr 'relax' position. Wolf's head was bent low, and he seemed to be deep in conversation with a tall, bespectacled civilian who looked as if he might be a clerk or a schoolteacher. So *that* was the 'sleeper'.

With a harsh 'Five francs, buddy,' the barmaid slammed the three glasses of beer down on the counter, and the Count paid for them. Seadog closed his eyes, downed his beer in one great gulp, sheer pleasure written all over his craggy old face.

'Better than mother's milk, mateys,' he sighed. 'Mind you, grog would have been better still.'

What were they talking about? Otto wondered, as the laughter, curses and shouts rose and fell all around him in the hot, sticky, steamy atmosphere. Who was the 'sleeper' going to finger for the killing? – for he guessed that was the shabby Frenchman's role. Otto's brow creased in a worried frown. He didn't like this business – not one bit. It was too late in the war to go knocking off enemy nationals. In the great days of victory they might have got away with it but not now . . .

A GI slumped to the floor, dead drunk. His comrades moving back and forth to the *pissoir* carefully picked their way round him, as if the prostrate body was a precious carpet. Staring over to the bar, Otto couldn't help noticing that the barmaid's right breast had slipped out of her low-cut dress. 'You've got a tit out!' someone yelled, but she didn't seem to mind; unconcerned, she went on serving, the white dug with its dun-coloured nipple almost drooping into the glasses of beer.

'What a cross-section of life, Otto!' the Count breathed, entranced by it all. 'What would the impressionists have made of it, eh? Lautrec or Renoir? *Un jour dans la grande guerre*, something like that –'

'Listen, Count,' said Otto, 'forget your great impressionists. Do you realize we still have a chance?'

'A chance to do what, Otto?' The Count looked at him curiously.

'To get out of this mess before the trouble starts. Don't you see – we could take a dive, even here in France. We've done it before, you know.'

'But the adventure hasn't even started yet, Otto!' the other man protested.

'No, but surely you can guess what the final chapter's going to be? A hangman's noose or a firing squad.'

'Noose? Firing squad?' interrupted Seadog. 'What yer talking about, my lad?'

Otto bit his bottom lip. Could he trust the old boozer? Had he just drifted into this ridiculous business through sheer bad luck or carelessness as they had done? Or was he a convinced Nazi, like the Zoo? Somehow he couldn't see the one-legged old bugger as a fanatical Nazi . . .

Otto decided to take the plunge. 'You heard what Wolf said yesterday. We're gonna knock someone off, and you can guess who it's gonna be. For my money, we're getting ourselves into something very dangerous, and at this late stage of the war, Mrs Stahl's handsome son Otto doesn't intend to have his turnip chopped off for a lost cause.'

'*Lost cause!*' growled Seadog. To Otto's alarm, there was suddenly iron in his voice, and later, when he came to think of it – *too* late, as it turned out – he could have sworn that the old sailor's ravaged, craggy face was animated by a sudden, burning hatred.

But before Seadog could say another word, a blast of icy air swept into the café as the black-out curtain was flung back imperiously and a harsh voice commanded, '*OK, let's see that ID, guys! The snowdrops are here!*'

'A raid . . . It's a police raid!' someone shouted.

Immediately there was a mad scramble to the back exit. A woman gave a little shriek, stifled the next moment. Hastily the barmaid thrust back her breast, as if the white-helmeted military policemen crowding in through the door might arrest it. A GI kicked the drunk on the floor and in a stage whisper urged, 'For Chrissake, Al, get up . . . It's the goddam law.'

Al, however, snored on.

'Let's see them dog-tags as well,' the tough MP sergeant ordered, as more and more helmeted military policemen poured in, grease-guns at the ready. 'Start lining up now!'

Otto saw immediately that this was no routine check-up; there were far too many bulls for that. They were in trouble. Their identity documents would never stand up to close scrutiny. He flashed a look at Wolf and saw that he had come to the same conclusion. His face was tense and set, and he was clutching his pistol under the table.

Otto nudged the Count. 'Get ready to go,' he hissed, as more and more of the GIs started to move towards the door, opening their blouses as they did so to display their metal identity discs.

'Let me go first,' said Seadog, 'because of my leg. All right . . . *Now!*'

With a savage yell he hurled his glass at the big mirror behind the bar. It shattered in a thousand pieces. The barmaid screamed shrilly, and out popped her breast again. Otto caught a glimpse of Wolf flinging up his pistol to fire at the lights. A shot rang out, and the next moment the place was plunged into sudden darkness. Everywhere there were cries of rage and screams, as Otto, pushing the Count in front of him, punched and kicked his way through the mob towards the back door.

'*Los, Mensch!*' barked Wolf. He fired again. Scarlet flame stabbed the darkness. Someone screamed with pain.

'*Krauts!*' bellowed an angry voice. '*They're Krauts!*'

A burst of machine-gun bullets ripped the length of the ceiling. People flung themselves to the floor on all sides. A hand grabbed for Otto's ankle. He lashed out viciously and his foot struck something soft. There was a strangled yelp of pain and the hand released its grip.

'Here's the door!'

Otto recognized Seadog's voice. Somebody tried to grab the Count. Otto tugged him free and slammed his fist into the GI's face. He felt bone splinter, and suddenly his fist was warm and wet. Together, he and the Count blundered through the door.

'Down the alley!' cried the civilian with Wolf, in the heavily-accented German of the area. 'Follow me – quick!'

In a ragged, blundering bunch they pelted down the narrow alley.

'*There they go!*' cried a voice from behind them. There was an angry burst of gun-fire. Slugs ricocheted off the walls on both sides. A line of bullets howled off the cobbles, spurting blue flame. Otto yelped as a stone fragment stung his cheek, but kept on running, arms working like pistons, head tucked down between his shoulders.

Seadog flung himself at the wall immediately ahead of them. Otto had never seen him move so fast. Jaguar gave him a boost and he was over. 'You next, Count,' Otto gasped, and bent his back. 'Move!'

Clumsily, the Count clambered on to Otto's broad back and disappeared over the other side.

Again angry flame stabbed the darkness. Wolf swung round and fired in one and the same movement. From down the alley came a terrible cry of utter agony and the sound of a heavy body falling. Someone cried, 'Jeez, they've hit the sarge, fellers!' and the running feet halted.

The men remaining on the near side of the wall waited no longer. Desperately they flung themselves at the bricks. Any moment their pursuers would recover from their shock and set off again. Otto scrambled up with the rest, and a moment later dropped down to the cobbles the other side, his legs feeling as if they had been driven into his guts with the impact. He gasped for breath, completely winded. Wolf grabbed him by the arm. 'Come on, Tex . . . Keep going.' He dragged Otto along with him, pistol still clutched in his other hand. Behind them they could hear the MPs climbing the wall now and the screams and cries as the others emerged from the café. Everywhere lights were beginning to flash on despite the black-out. Soon the whole place would be on the alert. They had to make their escape before it was too late.

Now they were pelting down the street towards the jeeps, and Otto was already groping in his pocket for the distributor head. Suddenly the first shots from their pursuers began to whine off the walls on both sides.

'I'll hold them off!' yelled Jaguar, above the chatter of the grease-guns. He dropped to one knee and started firing. The MPs came to a ragged halt, pressing their bodies tightly against the walls or diving into doorways.

Otto slammed into the jeep. With fingers that felt as thick and as clumsy as pork sausages, he ripped open the bonnet and fumbled with the distributor head, while the Count and Wolf piled into the jeep. Behind them, Lynx and Seadog did the same.

'Start up!' Otto yelled.

'Jaguar,' Wolf yelled, 'for God's sake get in the jeep!'

'Coming!'

As the two jeeps burst into noisy life, Jaguar made a dash for Otto's jeep, while Otto flung himself behind the wheel and rammed home first gear. Only yards away, an American voice yelled, 'Come on, fellers, the sonsuvbitches are getting away!'

Angry fire erupted behind Jaguar. A petrified Otto could

see the tracer winging its way towards him like a flight of angry hornets. He ducked instinctively. Jaguar screamed suddenly and his pistol tumbled to the ground. Wolf gasped. 'My God, they've hit him!'

Jaguar had fallen to his knees, swaying wildly, as if he might drop at any moment, the slugs whizzing off the ground all around him.

'I'm going to get him,' Wolf cried.

'Don't be a damned fool,' Otto heard Seadog yell with surprising authority.

'He'll talk if they take him alive!' shouted the 'sleeper'. 'They have their methods!'

For a long moment, Wolf, his face contorted with horror, stood there in the front of the jeep, paralysed with indecision. Then he raised his pistol and, ignoring the bullets cutting the air all about him, took careful aim, almost as if he was back on some peacetime pistol range. He pressed the trigger. The pistol jerked. Jaguar gave a scream of pain. Next moment he slammed down onto the cobbles, dead, and they were roaring away into the night, tyres squealing in protest.

With sirens howling, the little procession raced through Nancy's Place Stanislas. To front and rear were armoured cars; between them, a gleaming, olive-drab Packard staff car, bearing the outsize silver stars of a general officer. Instinctively, the few French civilians still left on the streets of the beautiful 18th century Lorraine city whipped off their berets in salute. For although they couldn't see the occupant of the staff car, they knew who he was all right. Here and there, GIs out on the prowl snapped to attention and saluted. They also knew just how unpredictable the occupant of that car could be – especially when he noted any slackness. In his army, the dogfaces went into battle wearing neckties and with their shoes shined.

Inside the Packard, the tall, silver-haired general wearily

nodded approval. It was heartening to be shown some sort of respect after the kind of day he'd just had; refugees crowding the roads everywhere . . . The rear échelon men in panic, burning their secret papers, their trucks already packed ready to bug out at a moment's notice . . . And the generals back at Bradley's HQ in Luxembourg, wetting their lace drawers in fear . . . He had been even warned that the Krauts had paradropped a goon squad to assassinate him. All along the road to Nancy he had been stopped by nervous guards at roadblocks and asked damn-fool questions – who was 'dem bums'? What was the capital of Utah? and the like. The questions were supposed to sniff out Krauts in US uniform, but it was damned frustrating to have to answer them all the same. All he wanted now was to get back to his billet, have a drink and flop into bed.

With sirens silent now, the little convoy turned into the Rue Auxerre, where a villa had recently been requisitioned for him. As usual, his staff were waiting for him and he briefed them swiftly in the hall, his long face pale and drawn, bags under his eyes. They departed as soon as he was finished, and Meeks, his coloured servant, brought him the bourbon he had been longing for all afternoon. He drank it slowly in his bedroom, savouring the taste, mulling over the events of the day. It had now been decided that his Third Army would counter-attack by the 22nd December, the aim being to relieve the German pressure on the First and Ninth Armies under General Bradley.

He yawned, and drained the last drop of bourbon. It was time for bed. But first he said his prayers kneeling humbly at the foot of his bed: the man who controlled the destinies of half a million young Americans.

Suddenly the phone rang.

He was startled. He had specifically ordered that no calls save those of world-shaking importance be put through to him. 'Goddamit!' he cursed, all humility vanished now as he creaked to his feet. Who in Sam Hill's name was calling him at this time of night?

He grabbed the phone and said in his high-pitched, squeaky voice, 'Patton.'

'Georgie? The voice was that of General Bradley, his boss, whom he had just left at his Luxembourg City Headquarters.

'Yeah. Shoot.'

'Listen, Ike's coming up to Eagle Main tomorrow morning for a special conference on this business in the Ardennes.'

'With Kay?'

'Without Kay,' Bradley rapped.

'I once let her handle my pistols,' Patton said slyly, referring to the prized ivory-handled forty-fives which were his trademark. 'She liked them.'

'Quit fooling, Georgie,' Bradley said. 'This is damned serious. Be there at eleven hundred hours sharp tomorrow. Okay?'

'Okay, Brad, and don't forget your ID. The roads are lousy with roadblocks.'

'I won't, Georgie. Goodnight.'

'Goodnight, Brad.'

The line went dead.

Undressing, Patton flopped wearily into the big French bed. Outside, all was silent now save for the steady tread of the sentries on the gravel outside. Patton's trained ear told him that they had been doubled this night, presumably his security people were taking this Kraut goon squad business seriously. He yawned, grinning, and closed his eyes. One thing was for sure. If the Kraut killers could plant a bomb under Eagle Main tomorrow morning, promotion in the US Army would be substantially accelerated. They'd bag the whole lot: Ike, Brad, Tedder, himself, perhaps even Hodges and Simpson, if they had been invited – the Supreme Commander, his deputy, and all four senior commanders.

'The genocide of the generals,' he muttered sleepily to

the darkness, and repeated the phrase, savouring its sound. '*The genocide of the generals . . .*'

Yawning again, Patton dispelled that vision of the sudden massacre of the US Army's most senior generals from his mind. Slowly he began to drift off into an untroubled, dreamless sleep. As he would boast to his staff over breakfast the next morning: 'Didn't even have to get up to take a piss. Pretty good going for an old guy like me, eh?'

DAY FOUR: MONDAY, DECEMBER 18th, 1944

'Dear Mother, it's a bugger . . . Dear son, so are you.'

Old Army Saying

COMZ had gone crazy.

Everywhere in the rear areas of France, Luxembourg and Belgium, the roads were packed with refugees. It was as if every stable, shed, barn and garage throughout those countries had opened its doors to disgorge all the wheeled contrivances of the last two centuries. Sagging in the middle and weighed down with their owners' pathetic belongings, they rolled ever westwards, only to be confronted with convoys of angry soldiers fighting their way east to the front. At nearly every crossroads there were massive traffic jams. Drivers gunned their engines to prevent them stalling in the freezing morning air, honking their horns irately, while red-faced officers bellowed at each other, waving their arms angrily at the stupid sheep-like civilians, whose only answer was '*Vite, vite – les Boches*!' Bare-headed brigadier-generals were seen directing the traffic, pistols in hand, trying desperately to impose some kind of order on their frightened men. That terrible December morning, everything hung in the balance.

Naturally the white-helmeted American military policemen were everywhere. They stripped indignant nuns to check for the tell-tale red marks of the parachute harness – for everyone knew that the Krauts disguised their agents as nuns. They made suspect GIs rattle off the tongue-twisters of their childhood; '*Rotund Rosie runs around the ragged rocks*' . . . '*Thin Cecil thinks thistles thorny*' (it being a well-known fact that Krauts couldn't pronounce an '*r*' or a '*th*'. And the questions! '*Me Deutsch . . . Nix Amerikaner*!' the pale-faced frozen cannonfodder, called to them as they were herded off to the front, vainly hoping that they might be saved from what was to come by being arrested. But the angry MPs ignored the cries. Let the doughs jeer. The Krauts would take the piss and vinegar out of them soon enough, that was for sure.

Nor were the generals converging on their remote headquarters that morning exempt from stops and searches. After all, the Krauts could masquerade as the top brass too, couldn't they? General Strong was arrested and led away in manacles for the crime of thinking that the 'Dodgers' was a form of rounders, 'a game played by girls in the UK.' One of the MPs had to be physically restrained by his officer from punching the big Scots general there and then. 'Christ on a crutch,' he snorted angrily, 'them Krauts have a goddam nerve! Girls my ass!'

Bradley was stopped and asked to identify the capital of the State of Illinois.

'Springfield,' the bespectacled, long-jawed Army Commander answered promptly.

'Are you sure?' his interrogator asked uncertainly. 'I thought it was Chicago . . . Okay, I'll give you another chance.'

'Fire away, son,' said Bradley wearily.

'Er, where's the guard located in American football?'

Swiftly Bradley identified the player's position in the general line-up. 'Okay?'

'You're doing better,' the MP agreed, 'but I'll give you another one just in case.' He grinned down triumphantly at the General. 'Who's Betty Grable's husband?'

'Never heard of him – or her,' Bradley admitted after a moment.

'Never heard of the girl with the million-dollar legs! Jeez, some guys are dumb! It's Harry James!' The MP shook his head in wonder, but was obviously pleased to have stumped the general. 'Okay, on your way, General.' He didn't even salute.

As Patton fought his way through the roadblocks, his

face grew purple with rage, twin pistols clutched in his gloved hands. Obscenities, terrible obscenities flowed from his lips, and every time a roadblock came into view, he would cry, 'Crap on dem Bums . . . I'll plug anyone who tries to stop me . . . *Get out of the way, goddamit!*'

Eisenhower himself only arrived safely at Headquarters because he had correctly identified who 'Ike' was – whereupon the grinning MP had clicked to attention and asked whether the General would so kind as to sign his 'short snort' as a souvenir. With a groan, Eisenhower gave in, consoling himself with the thought that the unknown MP would certainly vote for him in the years to come, when he ran for President. This was a secret ambition which had helped him through many a bad day such as this in these last years, and which, if the truth were told, gave him even more solace than Kay.

Fighting the traffic, the weather, the refugees, angry, frustrated and not a little worried, the Top Brass neared their destination, converging on the remote French fortress from west, south and north.

The stage was set, the actors were almost in place. Soon the drama could commence.

'You see,' the 'sleeper' explained in a ponderous schoolmaster's manner (Otto had guessed correctly – the agent they had picked up in Thionville *was* a teacher), 'the main underground cable-link between the various enemy headquarters runs straight through Lorraine. It's tappable at half a dozen lonely spots. As soon as Obersturmbannführer Skorzeny did me the honour of re-activating me, I set about tapping it at once.'

Erich – as the sleeper was code-named – threw out his pigeon chest proudly, and Wolf snapped, 'Excellent, excellent!'

Otto, huddled next to the Count in the shelter of the jeep, craned his head forward. In spite of his ever-growing unease at the dangerous situation in which he and the Count found themselves he was highly curious about the intentions of this group of mad SS killers. Seadog, for his part, watched the sky, which was leaden and ominous, heralding snow before the day was out – and then gazed appraisingly at his two companions. But Otto didn't notice that.

'. . . So,' Erich continued, 'I've been able to read most of the radio traffic between Bradley's HQ here at Luxembourg –' he stabbed the map spread out in front of him – 'Patton's here at Nancy, Hodges' at Spa – and Eisenhower the Jew, who has his headquarters here at Versailles.' He stared around at his listeners, as if expecting applause, a dewdrop hanging trembling at the end of his long red nose.

'Excellent, excellent!' Wolf repeated enthusiastically, apparently oblivious of the freezing cold on this windswept plateau overlooking the town sprawling below along both banks of the river. 'And what's the latest you have to tell us, Comrade Erich?'

'This.' Erich cleared his throat pedantically, as if about to commence his favourite lesson. 'Early this morning while you slept, I tapped the cable one thousand yards back there, near the hill road. At four in the morning, the traffic was enormous. Naturally some of it was due to our glorious new offensive in the Ardennes. But not all. It seems,' he paused in a professional way so that no one in his class would miss the point, 'it seems that a great meeting is planned down there in Verdun, which will be attended by *all of them*!'

'*All of them*!' Lynx and Wolf echoed incredulously.

Even Seadog seemed impressed.

'All of whom?' asked the Count a little stupidly. These days, things were happening a little too quickly for his poor old brain. It often seemed that people were speaking a language that he only half-understood.

Erich swung round upon him, and the Count cringed,

feeling like a naughty little boy caught in the school lavatories doing something he shouldn't be doing.

'All the highest commanders of the enemy armies, Mex,' he declared proudly. 'Eisenhower, Bradley, Patton – the *lot*!' He spoke with such vigour that the dewdrop dropped from his nose and fell to the map, spreading in a miniature gelid flood over Northern France.

'But not the Englishman, General Montgomery?' asked Seadog quietly in the sudden, heavy silence which had greeted Erich's announcement.

For some reason Erich flushed. Otto stared curiously at the old sailor. Somehow he seemed to have changed subtly – grown younger, his voice harder and more precise. Wolf looked from the 'sleeper' to Seadog and said, 'Well, Erich?'

'No, he won't be there – I don't *think* . . . Of course, I can only tap the US Army's land-line.'

'I see.'

Wolf clearly accepted the statement, but something told Otto that the skinny middle-aged teacher had something to hide. What it was exactly, he couldn't say – nor did he get a chance to find out, because just then Wolf once more addressed them all.

'Gentlemen, comrades,' barked the SS man, breath streaming from his nostrils, 'our comrade Erich here has fully deserved all the confidence that Obersturmbannführer Skorzeny has placed in him. He has given us the information we need. Now it's up to us to make use of that valuable – no, *priceless* information. Comrade Erich, I thank you in the name of the German people for your assistance. I think now that you should return to your home. It's better that you know nothing more of our plans.'

'Yes, yes, of course, you're right – er, Wolf.' Suddenly Erich seemed to lose his schoolmaster's confidence and was strangely flustered. 'I'd better be on my way.' Yet still he hesitated.

Then Wolf understood. 'Ah, of course, your – er, little

reward. Naturally.' He strode back to the jeep, returned with a clutch of banknotes, whereupon Erich brightened up noticeably.

Ponderously Seadog rose to his feet. 'I'll walk you to the road,' he volunteered – and curiously, such was his new authority that no one seemed to question why he should accompany the agent, who was obviously in a great hurry to be gone.

'Thank you, but that won't be necessary,' Erich answered, stuffing the thick wad of French banknotes Wolf had given him into his pockets.

'Just a security precaution, that's all,' said Seadog. 'Come along, matey, we'd better be getting on.'

Taking Erich's arm, Seadog began to steer him down through the snow-capped firs to the little country road that ran north away from Verdun, while the others stared after them in silence.

Wolf waited until the two figures had disappeared among the trees, then turned to face them.

'So – we now know all we need to know.' He smiled at the serious faces of his listeners, his features set in a look of animal anticipation. Slowly he opened and closed his extended fingers, jaw hard, eyes gleaming fanatically, as if he were crushing the life out of some helpless creature. 'We have the lot of them all in one heap – and they're ours for the taking.'

'You're crazy!' Otto cried suddenly, breaking the heavy silence as the full significance of Wolf's announcement sank in. 'There are only six of us, if you include the Count – I mean Mex,' he added, suddenly irritated beyond measure at the stupidity of the whole damned business. 'Do you seriously think that we can get away with murdering the whole Ami High Command? *Eh?*'

'Why not?' Wolf said without rancour. 'Boldness, my friend, boldness always pays off.'

Otto fought to control himself. 'All right . . . All right, Wolf, have it your way. Perhaps you might take the Amis by surprise, catch them off-guard, even knock off these generals of theirs – Eisenhower, Patton and whatever they're called. But do you seriously think you'd get away with it? Heaven, arse and cloudburst – the whole damned countryside would be alerted! They'd hound us down like dogs. We wouldn't have a cat's chance in hell!'

Wolf opened his mouth to reply, but another beat him to it. 'So you think so, do you, Herr Otto Stahl?'

They swung round in surprise.

It was Seadog, holding the bunch of French notes that Wolf had given the agent in one hand, a short sawn-off trench-knife in the other. And its blade gleamed with fresh blood . . .

At eleven hundred hours exactly, the Eisenhower convoy started to grind its way through Verdun, round the circular memorial to the dead of 1916, past the *gare* and up the incline which led to the squat outline of Eagle Main, once the *Caserne Maginot*, named after the gigantic sergeant and French Minister of War who had lost his leg on the grim heights that dominated the town.

As soon as the column stopped, the grim-faced MPs armed with Tommy-guns flung themselves out of their 'deuce-and-a-halves' and faced outwards, weapons at the ready, as if they expected Kraut killers to pop up on the other side of that dingy cobbled street at any moment. But all there was to be seen was one lone, scavenging hound, which lifted its skinny hind leg and took a leisurely leak on the lamp-post opposite.

In spite of his grim mood, Eisenhower grinned. The MPs looked really disappointed – almost as if they had been looking forward to an all-out attack by some suicidal Kraut goon squad. Acknowledging the salutes of the sentries at the gate, Eisenhower and his entourage passed inside the barracks, the MPs walking backwards behind them, swinging their Tommy-guns from side to side.

The rest of the Top Brass were waiting for him in the low, freezing-cold squad hut. The only source of warmth was a single pot-bellied stove in the far corner, and most of the generals were still wearing their greatcoats, with army blankets wrapped round their knees. Eisenhower was grateful that Kay had insisted he should wear his fleece-lined long johns this morning – it really was hellishly cold. He looked around the circle of serious, frozen faces and favoured the assembled company with one of his celebrated ear-to-ear grins.

'Gentlemen,' he announced, 'the present situation is to be regarded as one of opportunity and not of disaster.'

Patton was first to react. He snarled, revealing his dingy, sawn-down teeth. 'Hell, let's have the guts to let the sons of bitches go all the way to Paris. Then we'll really cut them off and show 'em up!'

The pugnacious remark broke the ice. There was muted laughter. Someone called, 'Attaboy, Georgie!', and Tedder, the English Deputy Supreme Commander took his pipe out of his mouth, and said, 'There's tea for anyone who wants it, chaps.' Even Bradley managed a wintry smile. Now the great conference could begin.

General Strong, still smarting from his undignified arrest, stepped forward to the centre of the room and quickly outlined the full extent of the German penetration in the Ardennes. Now Eisenhower took over, wondering vaguely if Strong would ever find that lost key – he still seemed to be wearing the handcuff on his left wrist.

'George,' he barked, 'I want you to go to Luxembourg and take charge of the battle, making a strong counter-attack with at least six divisions.'

'Yes, sir,' Patton answered promptly.

'When can you start?'

'As soon as you're through with me,' Patton answered.

Eisenhower frowned. 'What do you mean?' Bradley and his officers shifted in their hard chairs, uncomfortably conscious of the fact that Patton was showing off again. A few of the British officers laughed. 'Typical Yank,' someone said.

Patton, however, wasn't daunted by the reaction to his remark. 'I left my household in Nancy in good order before I came here,' he stated.

Eisenhower absorbed the information. 'All right, when can you start?'

'The morning of December 22nd.'

The effect on the meeting was immediate and electric.

'Don't be fatuous, George!' Eisenhower snapped angrily.

Patton enjoyed the sensation of being the centre of attention. He took his time, puffing at his expensive black cigar. 'This has nothing to do with being fatuous, sir. I've made my arrangements and my staff are working like beavers at this very moment to shape them up.' He explained swiftly the troops he was going to use, then added, 'But I'm determined to attack on the 22nd with what I've got, because if I wait, I'll lose surprise.' He pointed to the map and nodded at his boss, Bradley. 'Brad, this time the Kraut has stuck his head in a meat grinder. *And I've got hold of the handle*!'

Now the conference broke up into little groups to discuss the new arrangements and iron out the details. Once more Strong took the opportunity to lecture the three most senior Americans and the British Deputy, Tedder, on the increasing danger posed by Skorzeny's goon squads, which were now reputed to be everywhere.

'According to the French police, German paras have landed at Port Marly, not far from SHAEF HQ. Another French report says that two hundred of them have come down near Bohain, and according to a third, two companies of armed nuns were seen dropping outside Valenciennes.'

'Hope they kept their skirts well down,' Patton quipped irreverently. 'They tell me nuns don't wear drawers.'

Strong ignored the comment. 'It really does look, gentlemen,' he persisted, 'on the evidence at hand, that the Germans are making an all-out effort to murder one or the lot of you. We really must tighten up security at our various HQs.'

'I say,' Tedder said, suddenly turning pale, 'that tea from the Thermos tasted a little odd. Please excuse me, gentlemen.' As he stumbled towards the door marked WC, he was already thrusting his finger down his throat in an attempt to force himself to vomit.

Eisenhower looked serious. 'You don't think they'd poison the water, do you, Strong?'

'They'd go to any lengths to knock you gentlemen out, sir. I mean, imagine the chaos that would be created if they bumped off the three of you.'

'Enough, enough!' Eisenhower cried, raising a hand. 'Do whatever you have to in the security field – Anything, so long as we can forget this damned Skorzeny business and get back to fighting the war . . .'

Seadog cleaned the knife and let them wait. Even Wolf was shocked into silence. Finally the one-legged sailor spoke.

'I suppose I'd better introduce myself,' he said, all trace of his former slurred speech vanished. 'My name is Klotz – Obersturmbannführer Kurt Klotz, Reichssicherheitsdienst – *Ausland*.[1] Been in it since '33, and before that the Abwehr.[2] But you see, the Abwehr lot were all gents – like you, Graf von der Weide.'

He nodded at the Count, and Otto realized with a sinking heart that the Seadog was the real professional among them. Unknown to them, he'd been running the show right from the start.

'I wasn't. So in '33 I transferred to the SS.' He looked at Wolf cynically, as if challenging him to remark on his reasons for transferring, but as yet Wolf was too stunned to say anything. 'Promotion came quickly in that bunch of greenbeaks. Besides, the old Reichsführer had a lot of

[1] Overseas branch of the SS's own secret service

[2] German secret service

sympathy for a chap like me, who'd lost a limb in the old war. These people who never took part in combat – '

'But what did you do to Erich?' Wolf stuttered, finding his voice at last.

'I liquidated him,' Seadog answered calmly. 'For security reasons. You see, at this present moment, you five are the most important men in the whole of the German Armed Forces. I'd say each one of you is worth a couple of enemy divisions. I wasn't going to run the risk of the slightest leak. That Erich of yours had been kissed on both cheeks, you know.'

'Kissed on both cheeks?' Wolf echoed weakly.

Again Seadog gave him that cynical, knowing smile of his. 'Sorry – jargon of the trade. Yes, he was working for us, but he was also being fed by the Tommies. Their chap Montgomery is awfully keen to know what the Amis are up to, especially Eisenhower the Jew. Erich was tapping the landline for the Tommies as well.' He shrugged easily. ''Course, I don't know for sure whether he would have told the Tommies what we're up to, but at this crucial stage of the op, I wasn't going to take any chances.' His smile vanished, and his eyes suddenly became hard and keen. 'Tonight, gents, we're going to change the course of history. Everything else must be sacrificed to that end. Is that clear?'

The others nodded their heads weakly.

'Now, I know that you, Wolf, had some idea of shooting the Top Brass as they emerged from Eagle Main. Too risky. The security would be too tight. No – this is how we're going to do it . . .'

Swiftly, he started to roll up his trouser leg, to reveal several small, waterproof packets attached to his artificial leg, looking for all the world like puddings – indeed, they did give off an unmistakable odour of bitter almonds.

'Plastic explosive,' Seadog announced. 'We're going to use it to blow up the whole damned lot of 'em . . .'

Otto and the Count crouched a little way off from the others, who were grouped round an excited Seadog, eating cold spam and crackers – their last meal before they moved out for the kill.

'You know, Count,' Otto whispered, approaching the subject indirectly in case the Count's startled reaction alarmed the SS men, 'I expect one day, after this mess is all over there'll be a lot of people who'll say the war was shitting marvellous.'

'I suppose you might be right, Otto,' the Count said politely but without much interest.

'They'll probably say that nothing they did before or since was ever quite like it. They slept with whores in black stockings in half a dozen countries, they slogged through Russian snows and African sands, looted foreign castles, pushed enemy bigshots around as if they actually counted for something – oh, a hundred so-called exciting things happened to them. I confidently predict, Count, that they'll still be writing about this war in 1964 – perhaps even 1984!' Otto lowered his voice. 'But I can tell you this for free: Otto Stahl had a noseful of war right from the start.'

The Count lowered his can of spam. 'Why are you telling me this, Otto?' he asked, crumbs of biscuit caught around his lips.

'Because, Count, if you're one of these war-lovers – which I happen to think you are – you're not gonna live to tell yer stupid shitting tales, unless you start boxing clever right now. Make the wrong move tonight, and you won't survive to bore your long-suffering listeners with that crap of yours about the Great Game!'

'Boxing clever?'

'Yeah – we've got to put our thinking caps on right smartish, and do something to stop them.' Otto hissed urgently. 'Those SS geniuses over there think they can bump off the Ami *Prominenz* and get away with it. I don't.'

Count von der Weide nodded his agreement. 'You're

probably right, Otto. But we can't just go off and leave them in the lurch. It wouldn't be – er, well . . . *honourable*.'

'Honourable my arse!' Otto groaned. 'Talk to me about honourable when those Amis start dicing off yer dong with a broken bottle!'

'Otto, you don't think they'd do that, do you?' the Count gasped.

'They'll do worse than that after what we've done to their big shots. They'll pound our pills to powder, shaft us with steam-shovels, rip our ribs – '

'Enough, enough, please, Otto!' the Count moaned. 'I think I'm going to be ill.'

'You'll be dead if you don't listen to me, you silly old shit,' Otto hissed. 'Right?'

'Yes, right, Otto,' the Count said weakly, hands now held protectively between his legs, obviously very worried by Otto's dreadful prediction. 'What do we do?'

'This. We've got to pretend to be for this op heart and soul. The others mustn't have the slightest suspicion of what we're up to. We'll go along with them – but as soon as they've set those charges we've got to sabotage them. It's the only way we can save our necks from the Amis' revenge.'

'Would they really pound our – er, *pills*?'

'Of course they would, you stupid old sod – with rubber clubs.'

'Oh, my God!'

'So we sabotage the plan, and then . . .' Otto's handsome face grew grim, and he paused, pondering.

'It's the SS, isn't it, Otto?'

'Yes – they're worse than the Amis,' Otto agreed. He threw a glance at Lynx, Wolf and Seadog in the growing gloom, their faces hollowed out to dark death's heads as they huddled together, hatching their plans. 'Those SS shits don't know the meaning of fear, but somehow we've got to outwit them – *somehow*!'

As always on such occasions, the Count's emotional

nature got the better of him. He hated to see his young friend worried. Impulsively he clasped Otto's hand and said encouragingly, 'Don't worry, Otto. I know you'll find a way out – you always do. You're a born survivor.'

Just at that moment Seadog looked up from his conference and saw them thus. He gave a coarse guffaw. 'Why don't yer give him a quick kiss, Otto? I won't look. Ha ha!'

Inwardly Otto raged at the remark. One day, he promised himself – and one day soon – it'd be Herr Kurt Klotz who'd be doing the kissing.

Kissing my sodding arse!

DAY FIVE: TUESDAY, DECEMBER 19th, 1944

'On this day, four Germans in one of our jeeps, dressed in American uniforms, were spotted. Three were killed and one died suddenly.'

General Patton

Already the snow was beginning to settle, and the stone *poilus*, symbolizing the heroic defenders of this northern town, were beginning to look as they might well have looked nearly three decades before, when the Bavarian stormtroops had first appeared out of the whirling white gloom. But this latest group of German attackers had no time for history: with their footsteps muffled by the falling snow, they hurried from statue to statue, attaching a lethal packet of plastic explosive to each one.

Seadog was keeping watch at the corner, where the Ami convoy would have to slow down in order to negotiate the sharp bend.

'Use the red fuse,' he ordered. 'It'll give us half an hour's detonating time.'

Wolf nodded and, working in almost total darkness, moved from bomb to bomb, tying the fuses by feel, carefully assisted by Otto, who followed him closely, as if afraid they might get separated in the darkness.

Now it was nearly half-past twelve, and they moved fast, conscious of the fact that the Allied Top Brass attending the great conference must have finished their dinner now. Already a military police patrol in a six-wheeled armoured car had cruised down to the crossroads from Verdun, the searchlight mounted on the turret sweeping from side to side, searching the shadows for any sign of danger. Soon the *Prominenz* would be on its way, before the generals branched off here for their various destinations.

'We're almost finished,' hissed Wolf, wiping the snowflakes from his face. Behind him, Otto seemed to be attempting to cover the detonators with snow, although they were already virtually invisible. 'What now, Seadog?'

'Over there.' Seadog indicated the little snow-covered park, adorned by two rusting 75mm rapid-firing cannon from the battle that had been fought here in 1916. 'That'd be a good vantage point. We'll get a splendid view of the end of the Ami High Command from there.' He chuckled throatily. 'Do you know, they picked the French unknown soldier from the corpses they found here after World War One? They might have included my leg – I lost it somewhere round here.' He chuckled again – it wasn't a pleasant sound. 'This time, though, there won't be enough left of them to pick up the unknown prick, will there, comrades?'

Suppressing his distaste, Wolf sniggered hesitantly to please his new superior. 'Suppose you're right, Seadog.'

'All right, come on.' Seadog's voice had iron in it now. 'Stick close to me, the lot of you – and if anything goes wrong, I intend to use this.'

Otto edged closer and could just make out the pistol in Seadog's hand, to which he appeared to be fitting a grenade.

'What's that?' he asked. The old SD man had more tricks up his sleeve than a whore's pooch had fleas!

'Latest SD secret weapon,' grunted Seadog. 'Developed by the toy shop – that's what we call the boffins who think up these things. You know – rifles that fire round corners, silent electric guns, poisoned umbrellas, and so on. It's silenced and it fires a grenade fifty metres. It's like carrying a Stuka dive-bomber around in yer pocket.'

Count von der Weide gasped. The SD man knew simply everything. How would they ever be able to stop a man like that? It was impossible.

Crouched low, they hid in the little park that had once echoed to the din of battle, the snow falling sadly all around them, deadening virtually all sound, the monument to the *poilus* of Verdun slowly disappearing beneath the white flakes.

'Did yer know,' asked Seadog, trying to wile away time, 'they've got the world's biggest boneyard up there on the heights? A hundred thousand skeletons of men who died in the battle and were never identified. I reckon it's the biggest source of dogfood in Europe. If somebody would only – '

The words died on his lips. For suddenly, from the direction of the town, came the first low whine of a motor in low gear.

'It's them!' Wolf hissed.

'Yes, it has to be,' Seadog agreed, his tale of the old war forgotten now. 'Stand by. As soon as we know for certain, head for the jeeps – but wait for me. Remember, I'm not too fast on this 'ere peg-leg.'

'Of course we will, Seadog,' Wolf said, with genuine emotion in his voice. 'We wouldn't desert a comrade like you, now would we?'

Inwardly Otto snorted. What blind fools Wolf and his running-mate Lynx were. The cunning old bastard from the SD was in this for what he could get out of it. Probably they'd told him back at HQ that they'd double his pension or something. Seadog was that kind. He'd served the Kaiser loyally enough, then the Weimar Republic, now Hitler. One day soon he'd be serving whoever took over post-war Germany in the same way – even if it was Joe Stalin, the Red Terror, himself.

The noise got louder. Now they could see the glare of a searchlight at the head of the convoy, sweeping the snowy street ahead.

Otto felt a vein at his temple begin to tic nervously. Next to him, the Count prayed. Otto grabbed his arm and pressed hard, hoping he hadn't forgotten their plan; then he let go and concentrated on the ugly weapon that the Seadog held ready. He had to nobble him, too. God, he only hoped that the old bastard hadn't any more tricks up his sleeve. Or up his leg, come to that!

Just then the first armoured car swung round the corner, dark shadows silhouetted against the glare of the searchlight on its turret.

'Duck!' Seadog commanded hurriedly.

In the nick of time they bent to the snowy ground. In the same instant, the ice-white beam swept just over where their heads had been.

Now another long, olive-coloured car started to crawl round the corner after the first one. A flag flew at the bonnet, and silver stars were attached to its radiator.

'*It's them!*' Seadog hissed triumphantly. '*Here we go!*'

He raised his pistol. Otto licked his suddenly parched lips and tensed his muscles, ready for what was to come. In front of him, Wolf squinted against the falling snow, hands clutching the little detonator which would blow the American *Prominenz* into the next world.

Now the only sound was the beating of their own hearts and the snarl of the engines a hundred metres away, as the convoy of Packards, flanked now by helmeted outriders wrestling to control their skidding, sliding bikes on the fresh snow, slowed to a crawl to negotiate the sharp bend.

Another six-wheeled armoured car came into view.

'It's the end of the convoy,' said Seadog. 'All right, Wolf – *now!*'

'*Sieg Heil!*' whispered Wolf.

'*Sieg Heil!*' echoed Lynx.

With a grunt of triumph, Wolf pushed home the plunger.

Nothing happened.

'*Gott im Himmel!*' he cursed.

'Try again!' Seadog rasped hurriedly. 'Quick, man . . . They're beginning to pass the monument!'

Wolf fumbled with the controls, gasped and thrust the plunger down once more. Again there was no reaction – which wasn't surprising, for Otto had neatly removed each fuse wire immediately after Wolf had inserted it.

'Here let me, Seadog – '

It was the chance Otto had been waiting for. His hand chopped down. Seadog yelped with pain. The pistol tumbled to the snow. Lynx sprang to his feet, pistol blazing. In an instant all was noise, confusion, the bark of orders and counter-orders in English and German.

Suddenly one of the outriders had spotted them and was racing towards them, flat out. Wolf fired. The driver threw up his hands dramatically. The machine careened to the left and slammed into the monument. To the rear, the searchlight spun round, its dazzling white beam pinning them to the trees. 'Stake out!' a harsh voice yelled in English. 'For Chrissake, *do* something!'

The Count flung up his hands as Otto had ordered. '*We surrender* –' he began. Next moment, Wolf kneed him and he went reeling backwards, just as Wolf took the first wild bursts of machine-gun fire in his guts and went reeling round and round to disappear into the whirling gloom.

'*Count!*' Otto cried desperately, as another burst of bullets ripped past, inches from his head.

'*Otto . . . Otto . . .*' That last, desperate appeal seemed to go on for ever, until something heavy slammed down on the back of Otto's head and he started to sink with infinite slowness, red and white stars exploding in crazy confusion in front of his rolling eyes.

'*Otto*! . . .'

The swarthy US major with the golden sphinx of the US Counter-Intelligence Corps on his collar pushed the canteen of coffee towards Otto. 'It won't do your head much good, but it'll improve your nerves. I put a slug of bourbon in it.'

'Thanks,' Otto said, taking his hand off his bandaged head. 'It feels as if somebody stomped on me with hobnailed boots.'

'They did,' the major answered. 'Some Frog fell feet-first on your head. Now he's asking for the Bronze Star and two cartons of Lucky Strike for saving General Eisenhower's life. The General says he can have the medal, but he won't get the Strikes. The General's strictly against Class Six and PX stuff being given to the Frogs.'

'I see,' Otto said, sipping the steaming-hot coffee. 'Tell me. Where exactly am I?'

'Hotel Alpha, Luxembourg City – General Bradley's HQ. I had you brought here as soon as you were recognized.' The Major smiled encouragingly at Otto. 'By the way, my name's Cowen. Of course, you don't recognize me – but I do you. You were at our HQ in Algiers last year[1] when you were working for us. I see you're still at the same game. Thank God, you sabotaged those plastic explosive bombs! God knows what might have happened if you hadn't.' He frowned. 'Can't seem to find any trace of you working for one of our Intelligence agencies, though – but no matter, you did the job.'

'Where's the Count . . . and the others?' Otto managed to break in, feeling absolutely miserable, wishing he could rest his aching head down and sleep for the next thousand years.

'Count? We found no Count – or anyone else for that matter: they all managed to escape in the confusion. We did manage to lay our hands on the one who got hit, though.'

'Wolf.'

'Is that his name?' Cowen asked. 'He's not telling us anything.' He pressed the bell-push on his desk. 'Good. Perhaps you can get something out of him, Otto. You don't mind if I use your old code-name, do you?'

'No, just as long as you give me another slug of that sauce,' Otto answered. 'Anything to deaden the pain of my lousy head.'

Hurriedly the other man complied, pouring a generous

[1] See *Otto and the Yanks* for further details.

slug into Otto's outstretched canteen, while slow feet outside heralded the approach of Wolf.

There was a knock on the door.

Hurriedly, Cowen pressed another button. A green light started to glow over the door, instead of the previous red one. 'Read about it in a book on the British Secret Service called *Fifty Amazing Secret Service Adventures*,' Cowen explained. 'Apparently their chief's got one. I thought it was kinda cute.'

A soldier with a Red Cross armband opened the door. Two more followed, bearing Wolf, who was lying on a stretcher, covered with a blanket. It was immediately obvious to Otto that the SS officer was dying.

Most of the time they had been together, Otto had hated the hard-faced SS man, but now that he was dying, his heart went out to him. Suddenly Wolf's face had lost that fanatical, animal look; it had grown soft and somehow younger.

With an effort, Wolf raised his head level with the Red Cross man holding the plasma bottle.

Don't tell them anything, Otto,' he said weakly. 'Don't . . .' He groaned and fell back, exhausted by the effort. 'Promise . . .'

'I promise.' Otto looked at Cowen.

The latter shook his head. 'Not a chance,' he said softly.

'Wolf,' Otto said gently, 'did you see what happened to Seadog and the Count – I mean Mex?'

'They got away . . .'

'And?'

'Next time they will not fail.' Suddenly tears flooded the dying man's eyes. 'Otto . . . when we've won the war and you get back to Germany, tell my mother I fought bravely to the end . . .'

'I will – when we've won the war,' Otto agreed, forcing himself to tell the lie. 'I will, Wolf.'

'You're a good comrade, Otto,' Wolf breathed, and closed his eyes.

Cowen nodded and the two Red Cross men turned, bearing the dying man outside. A moment later the door closed after them. Otto knew he would never see Wolf again, he would die as he had lived, believing that impossible National Socialist lie, his young life wasted in the service of a crazy, brutal dream that could never be realized.

'Shit!' he cursed, and glared at the American. 'Why did you make me see him?'

'I thought you'd like to pay your last respects, Otto,' Cowen answered uneasily, trying to avoid Otto's gaze.

'No, you didn't! You couldn't care less about Wolf. You *want* something from me, don't you? Out with it. I know you bastards from Intelligence. You can never do anything straight. You've always have to go about things indirectly. You probably even screw sideways!'

'Now take it easy, Otto,' said Cowen, holding out his hands as if to ward Otto off physically. 'Okay – so I did let you see Wolf for a purpose. It's just the way we do things. That's the way we're trained at Intelligence school. I guess the instructors think it's more sophisticated that way. Hell, you wouldn't want us to take a billy and beat the guy's brains out, would you?' He gave a nervous laugh.

'Shit!' Otto cursed again, and slumped down in his chair, his head throbbing painfully. 'Okay, what do you want of me?'

'Otto, we know what the aim of your group was. Now they've missed their chance. So what are they gonna do now?' He answered his own question. 'They're going to concentrate on one single member of the Top Brass. But which one?'

Otto shot him a gloomy look. 'Go on, tell me.'

'Patton's out. So's Bradley. Their HQs are small and security tight. The killers would stick out like a sore thumb in Nancy and here in Lux City. You can guess who it's gonna be?'

'Eisenhower?'

'Yeah, Ike – in Paris. Sure, we've put tight security on him – but he's still wide open, and the impact of his death right now, in the middle of an enemy counter-offensive would be tremendous. The moment he was dead, the Limeys would be demanding that that creep Montgomery should replace him, and a hell of a row would break out between Washington and London. It would be just what your Führer wants.'

'He's not *my* shitting Führer!' Otto snapped testily. 'But what's all this got to do with me? I'm just a plain working-class feller.'

Major Cowen tapped the side of his nose, as if testing it for resonance, and winked knowingly. 'Don't sell yourself short, Otto, old buddy. We know all about you. But you see, Paris is like a jungle. Back in the States, they have no idea, simply no idea, of what's going on there at this moment. Every possible crime, every possible vice, deserters everywhere – some say a hundred thousand, British, American, French, Canadian . . .' He sighed. 'They come from every Allied army – perhaps even from the Wehrmacht, too, for all I know. There are black marketeers by the battalion. Hell, in one stockade alone we've got one hundred and eighty officers on black market charges! Some of them had thousands of dollars on them when they were picked up by the MPs! There are whores there, working for the Commies. There are others working for De Gaulle, some working for the Krauts – er, excuse me . . . for the Germans. And all of them working against *us*.' Cowen ran a hand through his hair in the manner of a man who was being sorely tried. 'In short, security in Paris is *zilch!*'

Major Cowen walked slowly to the window and stared out at the station below gloomily. As he did so, for the first time Otto saw that the American was a walking arsenal. In addition to the forty-five strapped low to his thigh by a leather thong, he wore a combat knife stuck down the side of his boot, two hand grenades attached to his belt, and in a holster underneath his armpit was a small captured

German pistol. He looked as if he was prepared to tackle the whole of the Wehrmacht single-handed.

Cowen turned again and noticed Otto staring at his weapons. 'These? I guess you can never be too careful, Otto. When we were in England last year, one of their Home Guard jerks ran amok with a pike in General Bradley's HQ. Said us Yanks had been interfering with his daughter. After that the General ordered we should be armed at all times. Interfering with his daughter! Jeez!' Cowen mused, rubbing his jaw reflectively. 'She'd shacked up with every officer and enlisted man in the HQ! But she was a good lay all the same. Now, where was I?'

'Paris.'

'Yeah, Paris. Now, Otto, I've worked out a scenario of what this Seadog and the other guys will do. They took both jeeps with them. So when they get to Gay Paree, they'll probably sell them on the black market – that's the way the French Army gets its vehicles, you see. If they can't buy papers with the dough, no problem: they'll shack up with some broad or other and no questions asked as long as they keep her sweet. Then they start trying to infiltrate Eisenhower's HQ, waiting for the right moment – I mean, security can't keep Ike under wraps for ever. He's got to come out some time – and Otto, that's where *you* come in.'

Otto looked at him, startled. 'What do you mean – *I come in*?'

'Take it easy, Otto, take it easy,' Cowen soothed. 'There'll be no danger in it. And you *will* be living in Gay Paree . . .' He leered at the other man knowingly. 'Know what I mean? . . .'

'Oh, get on with it,' Otto said sourly.

'Well we've dreamed up a scheme for flushing them out, Otto, but we need somebody to be on hand when they show – somebody who can identify them.'

'Me?'

'Yeah.'

'But why should you expect me to want to work for you?' Otto countered. He knew he was skating on thin ice, but he was so sick of the whole stupid business that he was almost past caring.

Cowen frowned. 'It's not for *me*, Otto – it's for the cause.'

'Fuck the cause!' Otto said crudely.

'Think of your old friend the Count, and the danger he's in right now. Besides,' Cowen lowered his gaze, 'I *could* conveniently forget who you are and simply treat you as a German national dressed in the uniform of the United States Army . . .' Without saying any more, Cowen jerked his forefinger back and forth significantly, as if he were pulling a trigger.

'All right, all right, you don't need to draw me a picture,' Otto snorted. 'I'll help you.'

'I *knew* you would, Otto!' Cowen said eagerly. Opening his drawer, he pulled out two bronze bars with clips and leaning forward, solemnly pinned them on Otto's two shoulders.

'Welcome aboard, Second Lieutenant Otto Stahl,' said Cowen, and thrust out his hand. 'Congratulations, Otto.'

Otto groaned. They'd got him again.

DAY SIX: WEDNESDAY DECEMBER 20th, 1944

'The morning of December 20 was D-Day in our own SHAEF section of the break-through. Intelligence reported a suicide squad of at least three score Germans headed towards Versailles'

Kay Summersby, 1948

The Supreme Commander was picking his nose.

He sat slumped at the big desk in front of the furled flag of the Republic, his highly polished shoes resting on the desk top, cigarette in one hand, bottle of French beer in the other.

'A Major Cowen and Second-Lieutenant Stahl to see you, sir,' barked the heavily armed orderly, and closed the door behind the two men as both clicked to attention and saluted.

Eisenhower sized them up. Outside, the Versailles Headquarters at the Petit Trianon buzzed with activity, telephones ringing, typewriters clacking, radio address systems squawking. The German attack in the east was intensifying, and Supreme Headquarters was working at fever-pitch.

Stahl recognized General Dwight D. Eisenhower immediately. He was much paler than the year before in Algiers, but otherwise he hadn't changed, with his high, balding forehead, wide mouth and bright eyes. Today, however, the broad grin of 1943 had vanished, to be replaced by a worried frown. Obviously the Ardennes business was preying on his mind. Why otherwise would he be drinking beer at eight o'clock in the morning?

'Okay, at ease,' Eisenhower ordered. 'So this is the German you told me about over the phone, Cowen?' The Intelligence Corps major nodded, and Eisenhower turned his attention to Otto. 'And you're the Joe who can recognize these killers, eh?'

'Yes, sir,' Otto replied, a little over-awed by a five-star

general who sat with his feet on the desk, drinking beer. It could never happen in the Wehrmacht.

'And what'll you do when you spot them, Otto, son?' asked the General in a very paternal manner, taking his forefinger out of his nose at last and examining the result of his excavations with some interest.

'Well, I don't really know, sir . . . I thought that Major Cowen here would . . .' He turned a little helplessly to his companion, to find him shaking with silent laughter, the tears streaming down his swarthy face. 'What . . . What –' he stuttered, 'why are you laughing?' With a sudden rush of panic, Otto wondered if his flies were open.

Cowen slapped him on the back and at the desk, General Eisenhower reached over and striking a match on the sole of his shoes, lit a big cigar.

'Hot shit, Joe!' he said in delight. 'It worked! We fooled your tame Kraut!'

Cowen wiped the tears from his eyes and said warningly, 'Knock off that "tame Kraut" business, Charley! Otto's one of us now – one of the good guys, got it?'

'Sure, sure,' General Eisenhower said easily, 'anything you say, Joe.'

Otto, his mouth gaping open like a stranded fish, stared from one to the other in complete disbelief, stuttering, 'What ... what . . .'

Cowen slapped him on the back. 'Okay, Otto, don't flip your wig. The guy you see before you isn't the real Ike. We've got him sealed away in the Compound with his – er, chauffeuse for company, guarded by a battalion of MPs and a company of Sherman tanks. No, this smart arse you see in front of you is Second Lieutenant Charley Chatham, who on occasions makes a magnificent jump in rank from shavetail looey to five-star general.'

Chatham beamed at a bewildered Otto.

'You mean he's . . . a double?'

'Right in one,' said the bogus Supreme Commander.

'You see,' Cowen explained, 'all the big wheels have

doubles these days. Roosevelt, Churchill, Montgomery – the lot. Even your own Führer' – he caught Otto's warning look – 'even Hitler has a couple of 'em. Since the July attempt on his life, he's starting to go in for them in a big way, I hear. Charley here is Ike's.'

'Not a very good one,' commented the man at the desk. 'It offends my professional pride as an actor that I can't seem to get that grin of his right. I guess it's because Ike's got more teeth than most people. Why, I mean to say, when he smiles, his goddam face seems to split in half. But still I eat regular, which is more than I could say when I used to tread the boards.' He gave a melodramatic flourish and took a pull at his beer.

'Hey! Knock off the sauce, willya!' Cowen warned. 'You're gonna put on too much lard to play the part. Okay, Otto, this is the deal: we're gonna use Charley here to draw the rats from their nest. We'll choose a public place with plenty of space so you can spot them in time and give us the wire before –'

'Yeah,' Charley interrupted hastily, 'remember – it's my neck.'

'Okay,' Cowen continued, 'now this is what the General here is going to do tomorrow. He's gonna open a Frog orphanage. It's slated as a kind of publicity gizmo. You see, most of these Frogs are creaming their skivvies, thinking that the Germans are coming back, like in 1940. So the General opens an orphanage, in full view of the Frog Press, the newsreel people and all the rest. After all, in the last few months, the US Army turned a helluva lot of Frog kids into orphans for one reason or other.'

'Liberation, they called it,' Charley ventured.

'Please – no snide remarks, General,' Cowen said severely. 'So already we guess that the news is known throughout Paris and, more to the point, that your former buddies will have heard of it. Well,' he ended a little lamely, 'that's it, Otto.'

'And this orphanage is right in the centre of Paris?' Otto asked.

'Yeah, as a matter of fact, it's not far from the Place Vendôme. How did you guess?'

'And you're telling me I'm expected to pick out Seadog and the rest from a crowd of frog-eaters perhaps thousands strong, all of whom have come to see the Supreme Commander? It won't work, Major, it just won't work.'

Charley suddenly lost his cocky air. 'You're right there, Otto. Jesus H. Christ, how will he ever spot a killer in a mob that size?'

But Major Cowen brushed their objections aside. 'Don't you worry, fellers, with Cowen in charge, you'll come out of it smelling like a roast.'

'Famous last words,' said a pale-faced Charley, slipping down behind the desk like a sinking ship. 'Famous last bloody words . . .'

The Place Vendôme was a gleaming black mirror in the December drizzle. It was one of those Parisian days when even the pigeons huddled deeper among the gothic sculptures on Notre Dame to escape the persistent rain. But even the miserable weather couldn't dent the Count's joyous mood as he, Lynx and Seadog sauntered up the street in the uniforms of British officers of the Brigade of Guards – just one of the items they had been able to procure with the money for the jeeps sold on the black market.

'Days like this, Seadog,' he announced, 'start one dreaming of one's youth. They bring back memories of a world of innocence and security and freshness . . . a summer holiday world where anything might happen. Listen to those trumpets. They come from the barracks of La Pépinière, and do you know what they are playing? I shall tell you. They are playing "*Ta femme fait la putain, brigadier* . . . Your wife's a whore, corporal," ' he translated hastily.

Lynx, wide-eyed like a tourist viewing the sights for the first time, was impressed, but all that the Count got from Seadog was a grumpy, 'Hold yer water, Count. A feller can't hear himself think with you jawing away all the shitting time!'

'Sorry,' the Count apologized. 'Just thinking of my youth, that's all.' He fell silent.

A minute later, Seadog halted them. 'That's it,' he said, with a nod. 'That's the orphanage he's going to open.'

They halted and viewed the 18th-century building opposite, where the workmen in blue overalls were hastily adding a fresh coat of paint to windows and doors, while, above the door, two more were hoisting a French and American flag into position.

'You can bet he'll stop on those steps,' Seadog said thoughtfully. 'You know these Americans – they can't resist having their photographs taken.' He turned and stared at the buildings on their side of the street. 'What would you say the range is, Lynx,' he asked, 'from up there to those steps?'

Lynx considered for a moment or two. 'Sixty . . . seventy metres, I should guess.'

'Then the grenade pistol should just about make it,' Seadog said.

'Yes,' Lynx agreed, 'and you don't need to be too accurate with that thing.'

Immediately the Count forgot his romantic memories of the Paris of his youth and stared at the other two in horror. 'But you're not really going to go through with it?' he gasped.

Seadog looked at him coldly. 'What do you think?' he said, as they started to walk up the street again.

'But –'

'No buts, Count! This job has to be done. It's vital to the interest of the Reich. Now, Lynx, we need to get into one of those buildings facing the orphanage tonight. In the morning I'm sure the Amis will search the area and post security guards. But by then it'll be too late. We'll already be in position.' He smiled cunningly.

Lynx nodded. 'Exactly. My guess is that most of those attics up there are unoccupied. They've probably been empty for years.'

Seadog frowned suddenly. 'Attics, you say? Well, that makes it damned difficult for me, Lynx.' He lowered his eyes to hide his look of triumph from the eager young fanatic. Lynx had walked right into the trap Seadog had set for him!

'How do you mean?'

Seadog stopped and tapped his leg. 'The old peg-leg, you know. Once the General's been hit, all hell will be let loose. The only means of escape will be across those roofs – and with my one leg . . .' He shrugged, leaving the sentence unfinished.

Lynx looked at him proudly. 'No problem, Seadog,' he declared happily. 'I volunteer to do the job alone.'

Seadog smiled softly. 'You're a very brave man, Lynx. I shall make it my duty to see that you're suitably honoured when we return to the Reich.

Seadog pressed Lynx's arm in a comradely fashion, secretly delighted. So he wasn't going to risk his neck after all. Lynx didn't have a hope in hell of escaping once he'd carried out the killing. He'd use both of them, the young fool of a fanatic and the idiot of an aristocrat, and then he'd be off back to Germany to claim the reward that Schellenberg[1] had promised him – fifty thousand American dollars, and a complete set of forged papers. This time next year he'd be toasting his weary old bones under the palm trees in South America, while the Amis were busy castrating all the SS men they could still find in Occupied Germany. The thought pleased him.

'Come on, the two of you,' he said eagerly, 'let's see if

[1] SS General Schellenberg, the head of the SS's Secret Service.

we can get a decent grog at that dive over there. Then we'll take a look at those attics.'

Like lambs being led away for slaughter, Lynx and the Count followed . . .

The rain had turned to snow. The three men huddled in their blankets in the attic could see it falling on the skylight above them, slowly piling up there in a grey mass. To the Count, fanciful as he was, it was as if he was in some Arctic cave, with the snow beginning to seal them off for the winter. The sombre mood, the feeling of being cut off, seemed to have affected even Seadog as he sat there, nursing his bottle of black market French rum, while next to him, Lynx carefully cleaned the pistol with which he would carry out the great assassination the next day.

'Do you know,' said Seadog slowly, as the wind howled and the attic window was lashed with snowflakes once more, 'I was trapped in a cave at Verdun in '16 for over two weeks. There were nine of us. The first man who attempted to go out to have a crap stopped a bullet just as he was about to take his trousers down. I can still see him dying there with his pants around his ankles. After that, we did what we had to do in paper and threw it outside. When the paper ran out, we relieved ourselves in our hands. By then we all had the runs – you couldn't even throw the stuff outside. The three men nearest the dead one wiped their hands on him. The rest of us wiped them on the earth. There was blood everywhere.'

The Count listened, fascinated and yet horrified. He had never taken much notice of the Seadog before. As always, his main concern had been himself. Now he started to realize what made the hard, cynical old secret policeman tick.

'On about the eighth day, the water ran out. So we began to drink our own piss. I think after that we all began to go a little *meschugge*. I was hit about then, and when they brought me in, they said I was raving like a lunatic. That was the glorious Battle of Verdun for me, comrades.' Seadog took a stiff pull at the rum.

'A terrible war,' Lynx agreed, obviously impressed. 'I don't think my generation could have stood that kind of life – years in the trenches. How clean and hygienic this war is in comparison, eh, Seadog!'

The Seadog looked at the young SS officer contemptuously over the neck of his bottle. The man was a complete fool – thank God.

'Yes, I suppose you're right,' he said without conviction.

While Seadog was in this reflective mood, the Count once more decided to take the plunge.

'Do we *really* have to go through with this thing?' he asked slowly, while the window rattled and shook in the wind, and little dust-devils danced about the floor of the candle-lit attic. 'I don't think it would be *too* difficult for us to get back to the Reich now, the way things are. But after the assassination,' he shrugged eloquently, 'I have my doubts . . .'

Seadog regarded him sombrely. 'You're a fool, Count von der Weide,' he said slowly, thoughtfully. 'You always have been, as far as I can judge from your dossier, and you always will be as long as you live.' *Which won't be much longer*, commented a cynical little voice inside Seadog's head. *Not if I have my way* . . .

The Count flushed.

'Much planning has gone into this operation,' Seadog went on. 'Your comrades, Wolf, Otto, and Jaguar, have sacrificed their lives to help it succeed.' Lynx, still busy with the pistol, nodded his head solemnly. 'Now you ask me to abandon the operation. *Nein, Herr Graf*, that cannot be. And you should be grateful that I don't discipline you on the spot for even suggesting it. You aristocrats are all the same – degenerates and perverts to a man. Always have been. In my line of work I've come across scores of them, with their dog-collars, whips, chocolate pudding and all the rest of their piggeries. No wonder they call them belted earls. Pinning on false moustaches to naked girls . . .Ugh!'

The Count gazed at the red-faced Seadog in open-mouthed wonder. Did such things *really* go on?

'So, I'm giving you a unique chance to prove to the ordinary working people of our beloved Homeland that not all aristocrats are decadent – that they, too, are prepared even to make the supreme sacrifice for the Fatherland, instead of just wanting to ram bananas up innocent girls.'

'*Gott im Himmel*!' Lynx said, shocked.

The Count lowered his eyes, as if ashamed. 'I'm sorry I mentioned the subject, Seadog,' he said in a low voice.

'Don't mention it,' Seadog said generously. And he licked his lips, cheered by a sudden mental image of himself under those palm trees, sticking bananas up nubile naked black girls. 'Now let's get on with it . . .'

'So,' Major Cowen explained, as the olive-drab staff car nosed its way towards the Place Vendôme, its windscreen-wipers going all out as they tried to contend with the falling snow, 'we'll have a couple of bands. People always like bands. The Frog Foreign Legion have offered one, and the Limeys have promised to lend us a pipe-band for the occasion. The Limeys are very good with bands . . .'

Otto let Cowen drone on while he and Charley stared out of the window at the crowded street, which despite the snow was packed with marauding soldiers from half a dozen Allied armies. British soldiers in tartan skirts with fiery-red knees; squat Polacks weighed down with heavy epaulettes so that they looked as if they were bearing a yoke on their shoulders; bewildered, shivering black Americans, wandering around a little helplessly, hundred-franc notes held in the air to attract the attention of the local girls. For, as usual, the pavement-pounders were out in force – companies, battalions, regiments of them, standing in doorways, walking up and down as if they were on sentry duty, each one flashing an angry glance at her neighbour just in case she made any territorial claims, or simply leaning against the ornate lamp-posts, as if they were too weak to do anything else. Stockingless, perched on high wooden-heeled sandals, huddled in blanket-coats or skinny rabbit-fur jackets, they offered their skinny, war-worn bodies to the greedy hands of these men of many nations. Otto's heart went out to them, it was a hard life, giving knee-tremblers in freezing doorways, or dancing mattress polkas all night long at twenty francs a go.

Charley, sitting next to him in the back of the sedan, was also gazing at the massed street-walkers, though evidently his interest was more mercenary.

'Hey, Joe,' he broke into Cowen's long-winded account of the plan for the following day, 'does your slush-fund run to a bit of tail for the condemned man?'

Cowen stopped in mid-sentence and looked round. 'And what's *that* supposed to mean, Charley?'

'Well, Joe, you never know what might happen tomorrow. If that Kraut – er, German killer gets lucky, it could be curtains for the last of the great Thespians.' He lowered his head and gave them what he called his 'John Barrymore look'. 'I mean, a guy would like to go out with a bang, if you see what I mean . . .'

Cowen frowned. 'It's not authorized, you know,' he said reluctantly. 'I mean, what could I put down on the expenses sheet?'

'Services rendered?' Charley suggested, and fluttered his eye-lashes.

Otto smiled, forgetting the half-starved whores and his worries about the Count for a while. The old ham was quite a character.

Cowen considered for a moment. 'Well, I don't suppose it would do any harm going into one of the GI bars and taking a peek at the tail. I've got a couple of cartons of

Luckies in my AWOL bag I could sell on the black market. Then I guess I wouldn't have to put it down to expenses at all.'

'Bully for you, Cowen!' Charley exclaimed. 'And I'll throw in a couple of cans of butter . . . *and* a can of dried egg! We'll have a ball.' He nudged the soldier-driver. 'Right, James – point this vehicle containing three very hungry men in the direction of the nearest piece of poon-tang.'

'Officers' poon-tang, sir?' the driver asked gloomily. 'I only know where the enlisted men get theirs, sir. Don't know anything about officers' country.'

'Then I'll direct you, humble, long-suffering man of the people!' Charley cried grandly. 'Soon you'll see how an officer and a gentleman takes his pleasure. Proceed to the left at the square. And make it snappy!'

It was nearly midnight and well past curfew as the big Packard raced dangerously across the snowy deserted roads back to Versailles.

'So, she said to me, "*Mon général*," ' Charley repeated drunkenly, ' "do I have to do it lying to attention?" '

In the corner a happy, if very drunk Major Cowen was singing a jolly little ditty in Yiddish. Even the grumpy driver was whistling the Internationale and telling himself that one day the gutters would run with the blood of these drunken capitalist pigs.

Only Otto was silent, sunk back in his former mood of mild despair. His girl had been friendly and nice, even – for a whore. Still she hadn't managed to help him shake off his gloom. It was nearly Christmas, 1944, after five years of war, and still the killing was going on. When would it all stop?

When?

DAY SEVEN: THURSDAY, DECEMBER 21st, 1944

'As an individual, the negro is docile, light-hearted, carefree and good-natured. If unjustly treated, he is likely to become surly and stubborn, though this is usually a temporary phase.'

US Army manual on black soldiers in WWII

Slowly, with that famous arrogant step, the French Foreign Legion band marched past, the brilliant white *képis* of the bandsmen set at a cocky angle on their shaven square heads.

'Krauts, the whole goddam lot of them!' one of the officers on the steps hissed, and Otto noticed Major Cowen go tense with apprehension.

Now it was the turn of the British men in skirts, swinging their bottoms like the warm brothers back at the Lehrter Station before the war. Otto watched and listened in amazement as they pumped up the air bags that they held underneath their right arms, squeezing a terrible shrill, keening note out of the things.

'They say that they eat sheep's bladder filled with shit and oatmeal for breakfast,' remarked the officer on the steps, in an awed whisper, 'and wash the stuff down with warm beer and whisky!'

Evidently the crowds of watching French civilians were impressed too. They clapped and shouted and when the wind tugged dangerously at the bandsmen's skirts, many cried '*Ooh la-la*!' in alarm and apprehension, the younger girls thrusting their hands in front of their eyes in case they saw anything unpleasant – it being well known that the gentlemen in question wore nothing at all underneath.

Now the US troops began to file past. These were blacks from one of the COMZ service battalions, and they were obviously carried away by the weird wailing of the British soldiers in skirts. As they marched, they appeared to be improvising strange dance steps, clicking their fingers, making odd little jumping movements into the air, and shouting '*Sock it to me, Jackson! Attaboy!*'

Otto frowned. First the Frogs, marching along as if they'd messed their pants, then the queer Britishers in skirts, now the blacks and their strange, shuffling dance . . . How on earth could this bunch have defeated the Wehrmacht, with its iron discipline and majestic goose-step? It all seemed very strange.

Just then, the huge English drum-major bellowed something unintelligible, his face turning bright crimson and looking as if a mouthful of sheep's bladder filled with shit and oatmeal had just gone down the wrong way. Immediately the strange instruments died with a last, exhausted wail, and the black Americans shambled to a ragged stop behind and bowed from the waist – for which they received a round of applause from the delighted crowd.

A heavy silence followed, broken only by the cooing of the pigeons in the eaves high above the heads of the crowd. The drum-major in charge of the Legion band gave a barked command, his breath fogging on the morning air. The trumpets raised their clarions, left hands on hips. As if on cue, the windows of the orphanage were suddenly thrown open and little children appeared at each one, their mouths bulging with candy given them by American public relations men and waving miniature Stars and Stripes frantically. The trumpeters blew their fanfare.

Suddenly the crowd gave a great roar. '*Vive le Général Eisenhower!*' cheered a thousand voices, each one dropping the 'h'.

Major Cowen nudged Otto. 'Keep your eyes peeled, Otto,' he urged. 'It's now or never.'

Solemnly, taking each step slowly, a portly French general started to ascend the steps to where Charley was standing, fingers raised in the V-sign, a wide if nervous smile on his face, waiting to be ceremonially embraced. The Legion band played. The candy-sucking children waved their flags. The crowd cheered, and Charley, flinching a little as the portly French general came ever nearer, smiled and smiled as if his life depended on it.

Suddenly Otto saw a dark shadow set against the bright white of the snow-heavy roof on the opposite side of the square. A man was holding something awkward-looking and heavy in his upraised hand. Otto gasped. That night scene in the little park in Verdun flashed through his mind's eye. *The grenade pistol*!

He reacted instinctively. With a backward sweep of his hand, like a cop pushing away an impatient spectator, he knocked Charley off his feet. In the very same instant Lynx fired. For one fleeting second, Otto could actually see the black lethal egg of the grenade hurtling towards them. A second later he was diving for the doorway.

The grenade exploded in a vicious ball of ugly red flame. White-hot shards of jagged metal flew everywhere, and Otto could hear it pinging off the stonework above his head. The French general screamed shrilly like a hysterical woman. Otto gasped. The man's features seemed to be slipping down his face and onto his tunic like molten red wax, leaving behind something that looked like the inside of an overripe fig. As if in slow motion, the French general began to crumple to the snow.

In a flash all hell was let loose. Women screamed. The flag-waving children dropped the flags and ducked behind the walls. The Brass scuttled away to cover. The Legion's march ended in a confused mess of discordant instruments, with the drum-major crying in German, 'Arseholes! Play on! What will the frog-eaters think of us!'

Now Major Cowen was on his feet again, 45 in his hand, yelling commands to right and left as the sirens began to howl and police whistles shrilled.

'*There he is*! *On the roof*! *After him, for Chrissake*!'

Suddenly Otto found himself running alongside Cowen, battling his way through the screaming crowd, clawing and tugging a path towards the buildings opposite.

Ham that he was, Charley knew that he'd never have a

part like this again: he threw his 'John Barrymore' profile to the newsreel cameras, which were still whirring energetically. Who knows, some Hollywood talent scout might spot him yet! Even now it wasn't too late for fame!

Raising his clasped hands above his head just as he had seen the real Ike do many a time in front of his soldiers, he gave the crouched, panic-stricken crowd that huge many-toothed Eisenhower grin, feeling the muscles of his jaw creak with the strain.

The effect was instantaneous. The panic ceased almost at once. Someone started to clap. '*Vive le grand Ike*!' called another. Suddenly they were all cheering and waving once more, with the band of the Legion blasting away at the *Marseillaise* while the British soldiers in skirts put up some stiff competition with their strange wailing music. Ceremonially, Charley looked down at the dead French general and raised his right hand in solemn salute. The newsreel men loved it!

Otto and Cowen braked to a halt inside the dark, smelly hall of the apartment building, heavy with the odour of garlic and cat's piss. On all sides the tall, shabby doors were closed. There wasn't even a *conçierge* in the little glass cage. The building might well have been abandoned. But Otto knew it wasn't. There was an empty pack of Lucky Strike on the dirty stairs.

'Come on,' he said, 'let's get on to the roof!'

Together they pelted up the steps. Outside, the sound muted by the thick walls of the 18th-century house, they could hear the MPs shouting orders to each other as they surrounded the building. Otto hoped to God that if the Count was up there on the roof, he didn't expose himself. The Amis would fire first and ask questions later.

Hearts pounding, they raced up the stairs to the top landing. A faint, dull light filtered down from the snow-heavy skylight overhead. Otto sprang onto the wooden stair-rail and with a grunt, heaved upwards. There was a slither of snow and the skylight flew open. A blast of icy air struck him in the face.

'All right, Cowen!' he cried, already aware of the shouts from below, 'He's up there somewhere – but don't shoot . . . I don't want those bulls of yours killing the Count.' Then he was gone, wriggling through the opening onto the roof, grabbing hold of the fire-hook and crouching there to survey the scene.

Immediately his eyes fell on the footprints. They ran, clearly indented in the snow, from the next skylight towards the mass of highly ornamented chimneys some fifty metres away. Otto gulped. It was the right roof, and for all he knew, one of the killers was presently hiding behind those chimneys; but which one? He licked suddenly parched lips and cried, 'Count, are you there? . . . It's Otto here! Count – *answer me*!'

But there was no reply.

Down below, Seadog's hand was firmly clutching the Count's arm. He had watched it all, and now was overwhelmed by bitter frustration. Already the damned Ami General they had come so far to kill had been spirited into his Packard under heavy police guard, shaking his hands above his head like Max Schmeling just after knocking out Joe Louis. He could have wept at the injustice of it. Would he ever reach that coral beach under the palm trees and shove bananas up naked native girls?

'There he is – it's Lynx!' the Count's urgent voice cut into his thoughts. 'He hasn't managed to get down!'

Seadog looked up, as did several thousand people all around him. A khaki-clad figure crouched in the middle of the snowy roof like a cornered cat while, unknown to him, another dark figure began to creep around the chimneys fifty metres away, clumsy but deadly grenade pistol in hand.

Seadog grabbed the Count's arm once more. It was time

to go. The old square would be swarming with 'white mice'[1] in a minute.

'Come on, Count!' he hissed. 'This place is getting too hot.'

'But what about Lynx!' the Count protested.

'We can't help him now . . . *Los.*' Firmly he started to propel the other man towards the rear of the crowd, while above them, Otto began to move forwards towards the chimneys.

The Count and Seadog came to a side-street. A long line of two-and-a-half-ton trucks stood there. Obviously they were the ones which had brought the black Americans to the parade. Now they were deserted, save for one slim black GI leaning against the first truck. Clearly the rest of the drivers had run off to see what the shooting was about.

Seadog hesitated. 'Count, can you drive a truck?'

'I can try. Why?'

It's the easiest way of all. Who knows – the Frog police might well have thrown up roadblocks; but they wouldn't stop two British officers in an Ami truck. Come on!'

The GI, whose colour was more yellow than black, looked at them without interest as they approached, continuing to clean his nails with a long flick-knife.

'You,' snapped Seadog, 'get out of the way. We need your vehicle. This is an emergency!'

The man was unmoved. He remained where he was, staring at them with a cool, insolent face, which the Count now saw bore a nasty razor-scar down the left side.

'Emergency, eh?' he drawled, and spat drily into the snow. 'Not for this soldier, it ain't.'

Seadog hesitated no longer. Tugging out his pistol and keeping it covered by the open skirt of his overcoat, he pointed it straight at the man's skinny guts. 'Listen, black boy, you do as you're told. Get out of my way!' He jerked the pistol menacingly.

The black GI's eyes looked interested, but there was no

[1] Nickname for the white-helmeted US military police.

fear in them. Slowly, very slowly, with a kind of feline grace, he moved out of the way as Seadog pushed the Count forward. 'Hijack, eh?' he said, as if things of this nature happened to him every day of the week. 'If I was you, I'd take the last truck. It's stacked with jerricans of gas for the rest of the trucks. It'd fetch a lotta dough on the Frog black market.'

The man's expression had changed subtly. Seadog could almost see his brain working. Obviously the man was up to something.

'Why did you tell us that?' rapped Seadog, while from the direction of the orphanage came the first dry crack of a pistol. Time was running out . . .

The other man considered, rubbing his scar with the point of his flick-knife. 'Well, you two dudes might have a proposition that could interest me. I'm getting awful damn tired of the Service of Supply.'

Seadog made a lightning decision. 'Drive us out of Paris safely and I'll cut you in one-third. Say no, and you're a dead man – now!'

With a quick gesture, the GI slapped the knife closed. 'The name's Washington,' he said. 'You're on. Come on, let's get that gas truck, partner . . .'

'Lynx – for God's sake, surrender!' Otto cried desperately, as down below the MPs started firing as if they were on some target range, feet apart, one hand on hip, obviously revelling in the attention of the crowd. 'You're going to get us both killed in a minute.' He ducked instinctively as a slug howled off the stone work a few metres away.

'Get away, Otto!' screamed Lynx, the hysteria all too evident in his voice. 'You're one of them . . . Get away, I'm warning you!'

'For Chrissake, Otto!' cried Major Cowen from his position at the skylight. 'Let the creep go . . . The MPs'll get him down. Don't risk . . .' But his voice trailed away, for Otto was already moving forward again.

Hugging the snow-covered roof, he began to work his way along the edge of the guttering, knowing that he was in dead ground here as long as Lynx remained crouched at the side of the chimneys. If the SS officer showed himself, he'd place himself in full view of the white mice below, so he, Otto, was comparatively safe – for the time being. But he *had* to find out where that arse-with-ears of a sailor had taken the Count, even if it meant risking a stray bullet from the MPs' pistols. After five years of trying to save the romantic old fool from himself, he couldn't just abandon him to his fate.

Grimly he worked his way forward, feeling the icy wind buffet his frozen face and his bare fingers slowly turn numb. Once he slipped and went slithering downwards, flailing madly, to be saved at the very last moment as his wildly kicking shoes found a hold on the guttering below. For what seemed an eternity after that fall, his heart raced so wildly that it felt as if it might explode out of his rib-cage at any moment. It was only with an effort of sheer, naked willpower that he forced himself to go on again.

Now he was about ten metres below the chimneys where Lynx was hiding. Slugs were howling off the masonry to his front, chipping off the stone in vicious little spurts, showering him every time he raised his head. But he didn't dare stand upright and shout to the MPs below to cease firing: he knew he'd be overcome by dizziness and fall to his death. He *had* to do this under Ami fire.

Taking a deep breath, he levered himself upwards little by little, forcing himself to be calm, knowing that all it would take for Lynx to blast him to eternity was for the SS man to raise himself and spot him, spread-eagled there on the snow-laden roof.

Now the wind was whipping the snow into his strained, crimson face in cruel, icy flurries. Both his hands were bleeding where the rough edges of the tiles protruding through the snow had ripped them. His shoulder muscles were burning with agony. He knew he couldn't hold on much longer. The only thing that kept him going was his insane determination to save that bloody old fool of a Count.

Now he was a mere two metres below the chimneys, and he could see the thick encrustations of pigeon shit and the pocked stonework, riddled with bullet holes. One more heave and he'd be there.

But it was not to be.

Suddenly Lynx's face was there, ashen, wide-eyed, stiff with sheer terror, staring down at him like a trapped animal which knows there is no way out of the trap but death.

'Otto!' he cried, the wind whipping his uniform, as he raised that terrible pistol. 'I *warned* you, didn't I?'

Otto closed his eyes and prepared to die. Lynx couldn't miss – and those damned white mice below couldn't hit a barn door at ten metres.

But Frau Stahl's handsome son Otto was not destined to die just yet. In the very same instant that the pistol fired, launching the grenade that would blow Otto to eternity, Lynx's feet slipped beneath him. He screamed shrilly as the grenade went sailing harmlessly into the grey December sky, and suddenly he was hurtling down the roof at tremendous speed.

'*Otto*!' he shrieked, as he shot past the young man lying prostrate in the snow, slithering downwards in a flurry of white. '*Otto*! *Save* me . . . *Otto*!'

His scream for help ended in a sudden grunt. Somehow or other, just as he had plunged over the side, he had grabbed the guttering. Now he hung there, swinging back and forth wildly some six storeys up, with only his hands visible, the knuckles dead-white with the strain, screaming with terror.

Otto gulped. Lynx had just tried to murder him. Why the hell should he risk his own neck trying to save him?

And even if he did, would he have the strength to haul him back on the roof?

'Stay there, Otto!' Cowen cried from the skylight, as if confirming Otto's doubts. 'We'll get a ladder. Don't do it, Otto – and that's an order!'

Otto cursed angrily. Once more authority couldn't give a damn about *him*, only about what he knew or could do. Cowen wanted him alive so that he could identify the would-be killer, that was all. He gritted his teeth. He'd do it – the Ami could go to hell.

Gingerly, he started to worm his way round on the snow-covered roof. Below, the dangling man was now making little whimpering noises like a beaten animal. Fighting back the fear and nausea which threatened to overwhelm him, Otto began to inch his way downwards, face forwards, using the palms of his frozen, cruelly torn hands as brakes, trying to dig his toes in as best he could, his gaze fixed hypnotically on those bright white knuckles and purple nails clinging to the guttering . . .

Desperately Lynx hung on. Obviously he could hear the sound of Otto crawling downwards. Now he croaked, 'Hurry, Otto . . . *Please* . . . I can't hold on much longer.'

'I'm coming, fuck you!' Otto hissed through gritted teeth, the sweat trickling down his face now in spite of the cold, his heart beating furiously. 'Hang on!'

Now he had almost reached the guttering. He paused for one brief moment, staring downwards at Lynx's hands, with beyond them the white upturned faces of the gaping crowd. He move his right foot around tentatively in the snow, searching for a fire hook. Suddenly it grated against something metallic. His heart jumped with joy. He had the support he needed!

'Now listen, Lynx,' he said carefully, trying to control his hectic breathing, 'I'm going to take hold of your right hand. Got it?'

'Got it, Otto,' Lynx gasped painfully.

'Once I've got it, try to brace yourself against the

masonry and push upwards. I'll heave at the same time. It's our only chance. Clear?'

'Clear, Otto.'

Delicately, fear blurring his vision so that everything seemed fringed by fog, Otto released his right hand. Now he was hanging on at a forty-five-degree angle, held by the hook and his own left hand, his body pressed to the roof as if to a lover. Slowly, very slowly, trying to make no sudden movements, Otto's right hand reached forward millimetre by millimetre. It was like watching the progress of a creature quite independent of him.

Otto felt a faint shock as his fingers touched Lynx's. He gulped. It was as if he was about to attempt suicide. One false move and he, too, could go plunging to his death so far below. He forced himself not to think about failure. 'Lynx,' he whispered hoarsely, hardly recognizing his own voice. '*Now*!' He grabbed Lynx's wrist and yelled, '*Heave!*'

Lynx, his body trained by years of obedience to command, heaved.

Suddenly his face, ashen-white, eyes wild, wide and staring, appeared above the guttering, level with Otto's.

'Free the other hand!' Otto hissed, digging in with all his strength, his arm feeling as if it was about to be ripped from its socket, the muscles of his shoulder ablaze with burning, terrible pain. 'Free it . . . For God's sake, free it!'

Immensely slowly, as in some horrific nightmare in which one is pursued by the fiend and can only move at a snail's pace, Lynx's hand relaxed its hold on the gutter and began to slither up the snow towards Otto's, while Otto held on grimly, knowing that the slightest slip could spell disaster.

'Nearly there,' he muttered through gritted teeth. 'You're going to do it, Lynx. Just keep going –'

It happened in a flash. Behind him, he heard a terrible ripping sound as the fire hook began to break away from the crumbling mortar. Instinctively he pressed his own free hand down hard into the snow to act as a brake.

'*Otto*!' Lynx screamed. '*Your hand . . . Your hand*!'

Next moment he was gone, plunging ever downwards, that last, despairing scream echoing after him. Otto felt himself slammed sideways against the gutter, heart beating like a crazy trip-hammer, knowing that he had failed . . .

Otto sat huddled morosely in a chair, clutching a whisky in his bandaged hands. Charley was posing in front of the mirror, practising profiles, but for once his heart didn't seem to be in it. Even the normally ebullient New Yorker, Major Cowen, seemed strangely subdued as he stood near the big window at Versailles, watching the snow stream down. To him, and to the rest, it looked as if God on high had decided to blot out this miserable, war-torn world for good. The failure of their attempt to catch Seadog and the death of Lynx had affected them all. From outside there came the faint squeak and rumble of tank tracks. Now they had moved in a company of Sherman tanks to protect Supreme Headquarters, though the whereabouts of General Eisenhower himself was being classified as top secret. Even Major Cowen didn't know where he was hiding with his 'chauffeuse'.

Finally Cowen broke the heavy silence and looked down at Otto huddled in his blanket, his face showing all too clearly the ordeal he had undergone that morning.

'Well, I know who Seadog is now, at least, Otto,' he began.

Otto said nothing, but continued to sip his whisky miserably, sunk in his own gloomy thoughts.

'I wonder if you can get copies of newsreels,' Charley ventured. 'I'd like a copy of this morning's performance to show to my agent.' But no one was paying much attention to Charley this grey, awful day.

'The description you gave of his age, appearance, the

one leg and that name, Kurt Klotz – it all tallies with one of the SS's hired guns, a guy named Karl Konradi. He always uses the initials "K.K" in his alias.'

'Hired gun?' Otto queried without interest.

'A killer – one of several the SD and SS used outside Germany from '33 onwards to get rid of political opponents who had fled the Reich after Hitler's take-over in January of that year. Heydrich of the SD was the first to initiate the scheme.'

Otto nodded. He'd often heard the name before. Heydrich, or the 'Man with the Iron Heart' as he was called, had been assassinated by the Czechs and British Intelligence in Prague in '42.

'The idea was to silence the leaders of the German Anti-Nazi movement – commies, monarchists, pinkoes and that kind – so that their murder would intimidate the rank and file.'

'And how does this guy Seadog fit in?' Charley asked.

'Well, according to our Intelligence, he was brought up on the barges, so his cover story was always that he was skipper of an international barge. You know how it is here in Europe – you can cross the whole goddam continent by canal, even as far as Southern Russia, without too many questions being asked at the frontier posts. For Karl Konradi, it was an ideal way of passing from the Reich to Czechoslovakia and Austria in the east, or Belgium, Holland and France in the west, where most of the German pinkoes fled after Hitler took over.'

Otto groaned. 'And that's the feller the Count's with. *Himmelherrje*, what a mess!'

'Yeah,' Cowen said cheerfully. 'Apparently he's been on our blacklist for several years now. Automatic arrest category. He must have carried out at least a dozen killings in his time.' He slapped the butt of the Springfield rifle – he'd started carrying it that morning as an extra safeguard. 'But don't worry, Otto – he's definitely on the run now. All the cops in the COMZ, including the Frog cops, too, have his description and the Count's as well. The dragnet's out for them. They haven't a hope in hell of escaping. Friend Karl Konradi, alias Kurt Klotz, alias Seadog, has claimed his last victim.'

But there the heavily-armed US Intelligence major was wrong.

The breeze swept the bitter smell of *anis* and fried potatoes down the dark street. A sad song about a soldier who had abandoned his *petite fille* blared forth from a tinny loudspeaker. 'You like show? Like exhibition?' called the taxi-cab drivers as they cruised past. 'Special show for Americans. Plenty jig-jig!'

Down at the end of the street, a couple of men in heavy leather overcoats, with felt hats pulled down well over their foreheads, started checking the papers of the whores and pimps who congregated there.

Washington dug Seadog in the ribs. 'In there – that's the place.'

As they pushed back the heavy felt black-out curtain, the Count and Seadog stifled a gasp of astonishment. The café was crowded with noncoms and soldiers of half a dozen armies – and all of them were black.

The Count blinked as if he could hardly believe his eyes, but it was true: the only whites in evidence were the grinning French whores.

Washington grinned. 'You thought you was colour-blind, eh?'

They pushed their way inside. A dazzling yellow spot illuminated the sweating features of a black man dressed up to look like a Parisian *apaché*, right down to the beret, striped jersey and cigarette glued to his bottom lip, who was belting out Maurice Chevalier's pre-war favourite, 'Valenteene', to a thunderous accordion accompaniment. On reaching the words '*Elle avait de tout petits michons*', he drew the accordion out obscenely, and the French soldiers among the audience roared back, '*Valenteene . . . Valenteene*!' The rest, however, were more preoccupied with the raucous whores and their drinks. There was little sign of enjoyment on their sweating faces, just a drunken determination to make the most of this brief moment of escape.

Washington slipped five cigarettes to a hulking Senegalese waiter whose face was disfigured with ritual tribal scars.

'Usual table, Joe,' he said, with the air of one who knew the ropes. 'No whores, no pimps, no fake champagne. Three beers.'

'Okay, Washington,' replied the Senegalese in a deep bass, and guided them to a table at the rear of the smoke-filled room. Here they were to rendezvous with the mysterious Ami who was, as their new comrade Washington informed them, 'Mr Big – the guy who works the whole racket in the COMZ, a real smart operator . . . *Real* smart.'

The lights turned to a whirling green, and a young woman walked to the centre of the floor.

'I say!' the Count gasped. 'She's got no clothes on!'

Washington chuckled. 'That ain't no lady, Count!'

She started to dance clumsily, moving slowly at first, but getting quicker all the time, breasts shuddering, sweat pouring off her ample body, urged on by the audience of drunken blondes and black GIs, their faces glistening in the lurid, unreal light. The drums thudded faster. The applause and shrill whistles gathered to a crescendo. Round and round the woman whirled, until suddenly she began to break into great shuddering jerks. Desperately she ripped her clenched hands up and down her sweat-lathered body. Her eyes went blank. Her hair flew. Meaningless groans issued from her slack, wet lips. Legs planted apart, pelvis thrust out, she revolved her hips in a crazy circle, while her audience went mad, stamping their boots on the floor, yelling obscenities, crying encouragement.

'I s-say,' the Count stuttered, bewildered by it all. 'I wonder if the poor woman's ill or something?'

But no one was paying attention to the Count.

With startling suddenness, the woman dropped to the stage, completely exhausted. The music stopped. The lights went out. The excitement fled from the enervated spectators, and there was a sudden, uneasy silence, broken only by the woman's soft moans.

The Count cleared his throat nervously. Next to him, Washington murmured, 'Shit! Ain't *that* something!' as if talking to himself. Only Seadog seemed unimpressed. 'How much longer do we have to –'

He stopped in mid-sentence. Suddenly the lights had flashed on, harsh, white and blinding, to reveal that the woman had gone. In her place stood a huge black man, nearly two metres high and almost as broad, dressed in sloppy, rumpled khaki, his little dark eyes almost invisible in that vast fat face as he grinned down at them.

'These the dudes, Washington?' he asked lazily.

With surprising speed their companion sprang to his feet, his usual arrogant laziness vanished, indicating with an urgent movement of his hand that the Count and Seadog should do likewise.

Slowly they did so, and Seadog asked, somewhat awe-struck by the sheer size of the man, 'Who . . . Who *are* you?'

The big man laughed uproariously, his whole body shaking with mirth, his jowls seeming to slap each other like a pair of applauding black hands.

'Why, whitey,' he said, and thrust a thumb like a blood sausage at his massive chest, '*I*'s the *Big Nig*!' And immediately he went off into another mad peal of booming laughter . . .

DAY EIGHT: FRIDAY, DECEMBER 22nd, 1944

'M'sieu, the honour to shoot first is yours.'

General d'Auteroche to his British opposite number at the Battle of Fontenoy

The Supreme Commander's pre-Christmas party was a flop. Even the fact that the champagne flowed freely and all the senior generals had contributed their month's ration of hard booze couldn't save it.

The knowledge that the new German offensive in the Ardennes was gaining ground all the time and that the panzers were now moving steadily westwards weighed heavily on the minds of all present. American casualties were mounting rapidly, too.

In spite of the funny paper hats that Eisenhower had ordered to be distributed and the efforts of the Headquarters band, who were now swinging manfully into 'Little Brown Jug' and 'American Patrol' in a fair imitation of Glenn Miller, the talk was subdued and conducted mostly from behind a concealing hand. The rumours were flying back and forth rapidly, alarmingly.

Otto, who was leaning against one of the ornate walls of the big Versailles Headquarters, couldn't hear exactly what was being said, but he knew instinctively what the pasty-faced staff officers and the lumpy WAC clerks were whispering about: the threat to Eisenhower's life. The whole Headquarters had been turned into an armed camp, and even at this moment, the building in which they were celebrating was surrounded by thirty-ton Sherman tanks, as if Skorzeny might appear at any moment at the head of a column of Tigers, their 88mm cannon blazing.

Otto sipped his bourbon moodily and stared out of the window at the falling snow, where the helmeted sentries plodded up and down glumly, bent under the snow like weary peasants. With a stab of anxiety he wondered what had happened to the Count. Perhaps Seadog had seen sense at last – he didn't look the type to risk his neck for the sacred cause of National Socialism. Maybe even now he was attempting to get himself and the Count back to Germany while the going was good. He knew that was Major Cowen's theory. Unlike the rest of the top security Brass, it was Cowen's view that the threat to Eisenhower's life was over – though Otto couldn't help noticing that in addition to his rifle, grenades, forty-five and combat knife, the Major now also carried a two-inch bazooka on his left shoulder. Clearly, however, this made dancing somewhat difficult, for as Cowen and his heavy-bosomed WAC partner swung by, Otto heard her remark, 'Major, if that goddam bazooka hits my tits again, I swear I'll put in for the Purple Heart!'

'What about the Purple Tit?' Cowen chortled, showing rare wit for him. And then they were gone, and Otto heard no more.

Otto concluded he must be getting tight. He took another pull at his drink and tried to shake himself out of his mood of gloom, but it was no use: the way things were going, the war could go on for another ten years!

'Penny for 'em.'

Otto turned, startled, and then straightened up into the position of attention.

It was Charley Chatham, alias the Supreme Commander, surrounded by the usual côterie of hangers-on, including his red-haired 'chauffeuse', Lieutenant Kay Summersby. It was obvious that the one-time pride of New England summer stock theatre had been hitting Ike's special bourbon rather more heavily than was good for him. His face was red and his smile was too ready. He winked at Otto, and behind him, his Chief of Staff, General Bedell Smith, whose temper was reputedly as fiery as his hair, frowned disapprovingly.

The frown didn't appear to worry Charley in the

slightest. 'Having a good time, Otto?' he went on, without waiting for Otto to answer. 'Plenty of booze and broads, eh?' He gave Otto a dig in the ribs. 'Even if they do wear khaki drawers!'

'*Sir*!' Lieutenant Summersby breathed, shocked, and Otto heard Bedell Smith clear his throat noisily.

Charley was unabashed. 'Have a drink, Beetle,' he said magnanimously, slapping the Chief of Staff heartily on the shoulders. 'Ya sound like yer've got something stuck in your gullet.'

'Yes . . . er, Ike,' the Chief of Staff stuttered, while Charley winked and passed on, swaying slightly as he went.

'You're this guy Stahl, are you then?' said the Chief of Staff stiffly as the rest of the retinue drifted after Charley, who was now chatting to a blonde WAC and idly patting her bottom as he did so.

'Yes, sir.' Instinctively Otto knew that the red-haired general with the angry eyes spelled danger. He knew the type – the German Army was full of them. *This* one he had to watch.

'You realize that this thing is totally, absolutely top secret, Stahl?' rasped Bedell Smith. 'If the truth ever came out, it would ruin the General's chance of a political career after the war. The United States of America,' Bedell Smith deliberately used the full phrase, as if it had some mystical importance, 'would never tolerate a senior soldier-cum-politician who appeared to have been scared. Our country expects its leaders to be brave, decent, family-loving, God-fearing folk. Do you understand, Stahl?'

'Yes, sir,' Otto snapped back. Behind Bedell Smith, he could see that Charley's hand was now resting lightly on the big blonde's blouse, the fingers twirling the nipple, while the WAC smirked and the 'chauffeuse' fumed impotently. 'It takes a stiff rod to catch a big fish,' Charley was saying drunkenly, to which the blonde replied, 'But I bet you've got the stiff rod, General.' Whereupon she burst out into tipsy giggles.

'You're treading on dangerous ground, Stahl,' the Chief of Staff went on, unaware that Otto's attention was riveted on the little scene being played out behind his back. '*Very* dangerous ground. Let me say this to you. Keep your mouth buttoned up at all times about what goes on here.' He thrust his angry face closer to Otto's threateningly. 'Because if you don't, Stahl, you might find yourself in trouble – serious trouble. Do you read me?'

Otto swallowed hard. 'Yes, sir,' he quavered, staring back at those red-rimmed, dangerous eyes and feeling suddenly very afraid. General Bedell Smith, he realized, was not a man to issue idle threats. Put a foot wrong with this man and he might well find himself staring up at the potatoes from two metres of earth. It was something he was going to have to bear in mind for the future – if there *was* a future for Mrs Stahl's handsome son.

'Okay, Stahl, don't forget what I told you. Carry on.'

And so saying, Bedell Smith passed on, leaving a very worried Otto behind him.

Not ten miles away from Versailles, Count von der Weide was also attending a not very successful party, though on a much smaller scale – and he, too, by a strange coincidence, had suddenly become a very worried man.

It had all started innocently and harmlessly enough. As at Versailles, there had been plenty of black market booze here in the back room that served as the Big Nig's headquarters. There had been music, too, with the whores who frequented the café dancing to the scratchy records of *bal musette* music or perching themselves on the knees of the black soldiers from the Red Ball Express.

The Big Nig, his huge fat face dripping with sweat and grease as he wolfed down a mountainous plateful of pig's knuckles, had been in an expansive mood, too, as he reminisced about his past and the reasons for his desertion from the US Army.

'You see, gents, a coupla times as a kid I reckoned I was in for a necktie party, 'cos I'm a real black nigger and in cracker country, when the rednecks get bored on a Saturday evening, they go looking for fellers like me for a little whoopee. But later I graduated from Harvard.' He swallowed a big chunk of red meat and winked. 'Yeah – not only am I a real black nigger, I'm a goddam *educated* nigger as well! Two strikes against me, eh, gents?'

Seadog and the Count made suitable noises at this point, though in fact the Count had understood only half of what the Big Nig was saying. His monologue wasn't helped by the fact that he seemed to have half a cow in his mouth most of the time and kept breaking off to take huge gulps of frothy thin French beer – this, out of a glass which Washington refilled constantly from a pail on the floor.

'Still,' he continued, poking at his teeth with his gem-laden little finger, to dislodge a chunk of meat, 'when the Nips hit Pearl Harbor, it was my country right or wrong. I volunteered for the Service like some hotshot Georgia cracker. I shoulda known better. So where did Uncle Sam send this educated nigger? I'll tell you, gents – straight back to cracker country!' He shook his huge head and the jowls slapped back and forth, showering his listeners with drops of sweat. 'Brother, wasn't that something! Crackers refusing the soldiers of the Army of the Republic, sworn to defend them, a drink of goddam water – all 'cos they were black. Crackers shooting up nigger camps of a Saturday night. Crackers cutting the dick off some poor nigger GI 'cos he looked at a white gal.' He gulped for breath and his enormous stomach jerked up his gigantic frame. 'Hell, *them crackers treated Nazi POWs better than they did their own black soldiers*!'

As the Big Nig spoke, the Count began to realize that underneath his easy-going fat man's bonhomie, there was a burning, bitter sense of injustice.

'Gents, it was like the Day of Jubilation, the day the US of A posted this poor old nigger boy overseas,' the Big Nig continued, sucking the end of the pig's knuckle, his thick, dark-red lips running with grease. 'I coulda gone down on my knees and kissed the deck of that Limey ship.' He chuckled throatily. 'I was freed of the crackers at last – leastways, that's what I thought.'

Washington poured him another glass of beer from the pail, and he accepted it with dignity; it was almost as if he were a king of this strange, flourishing underworld empire in the midst of wartime Paris. 'Of course, the Limeys were okay. There was no prejudice in them – until they started meeting our own democratic freedom-loving American crackers. So it was about then that the Big Nig – who, in another life, was Technical Sergeant Abe-Lincoln Lee Stuart – decided that he had to sever his association with the Army of the Republic. In other words, gents, I went over the hill.'

'Over the hill?' Seadog queried, somewhat alarmed by the way the Big Nig was running off at the mouth. He had nothing against black people – for him, they were no different from the Macaroni-Eaters, the Cheeseheads, Popovs, Frogs and all the rest. But all the same he preferred them to be seen and not heard.

'Deserted,' said Washington, acting as interpreter for the Big Nig, whom he obviously admired.

'Thank you, Washington,' said Big Nig, with a majestic sweep of his huge black paw. 'Yeah, so I went AWOL and took over the Red Ball Express set-up.' Seeing the puzzled look on the faces of his two white listeners, he realized that a little explanation was called for. 'See, ever since the D-Day landings, General Ike's had a truck supply route from the beaches to the front, carrying up gas, smokes, rations, ammo and the like. No other vehicles are allowed to use it. Now, the Red Ball Express runs twenty-four hours a day, seven days a week.' He smiled hugely at them. 'Every day that dawns, a couple of million bucks in black market goodies goes up those roads, gents, driven by black soldiers – and gents, *the Big Nig controls those black soldiers*! By Christmas, I'm gonna be a dollar millionaire. And if this goddam war lasts long enough, the poor old Big Nig's gonna retire with enough dough to paper the White House three times over!'

With a satisfied smile, the big black man lounged back in his chair, eyes narrowed to slits, and undid a trouser button to allow more room for his enormous belly, bloated by the food and beer.

But the Count wasn't entirely convinced. Behind those narrowed eyes, he sensed an active brain, racing swiftly, attempting to sum them up, asking itself why these two middle-aged white men, dressed absurdly in the uniform of the British Guards, had come to see him.

'So you see, gents, the Big Nig has developed into an *entrepreneur, par excellence*. You wanna broad in your slit trench? I get you a broad. You want some fake ID to get you out the goddam line? I get it. You want some officer-style bourbon? Can do!' He spread his big pink palms outwards in the manner of a satisfied businessman. 'Guess my old mammy must have had a roll in the hay with old Abie Rosenshit. Must have Jewish blood in my poor black body.' And once more he trembled with laughter.

But those slit-like eyes weren't laughing one bit.

Tentatively, Washington decided it was time to explain to the Big Nig their reason for being there. 'Er, boss . . . Me and these white folks here,' he commenced, checking if the Big Nig's glass was still filled with beer, 'have got a deuce-and-a-half and fifty jerricans of gas that we want to do a deal on, Big Nig. We thought you was the proper guy to come to . . .' Anxiously he looked up for approval.

'And you did right, son,' the Big Nig agreed heartily, his eyes remaining glued on the white men. 'And may I ask what you want in exchange for the truck and the gas?'

'Money,' ventured Seadog. 'Enough money to get us out

of this place. Washington here wants to go to London. We want to go – er, somewhere else.'

'Somewhere else, eh?' mused the Big Nig, and the Count had the distinct and uncomfortable impression the huge black man was toying with them. Somehow he had already guessed who they were and what they were *really* after: a quick return to the Reich.

'Yes, we're on the run,' Seadog added hastily.

'On the run, eh?' the Big Nig echoed, face gentle in repose as he stroked his triple chins thoughtfully. 'You don't say. Are you deserters from the Limey army, perhaps?'

Seadog jumped at the suggestion. 'Yes, that's it!' he responded eagerly. 'We're deserters from the British Army.'

Slowly, deliberately, the Big Nig laughed, while Washington stared, bewildered, from him to the white men, who both waited uneasily for what was to come. 'Hell, gents, you trying to pull my pisser? Don't you know the word's out on you two? Every cop in the COMZ's looking for you guys.' His laugh ended abruptly. 'What you done?' he rapped, authority in his husky voice now. 'Come on, spit it out!'

For once, the Count took the initiative. All around him the laughing whores and black men had fallen silent. On the gramophone the old record whirled round and round scratchily. Suddenly there was menace in the air. Everyone was looking at them.

'We're – er, German prisoners of war,' he lied glibly. 'We escaped from Cherbourg cage and we're trying to get back to Germany . . .'

'Kraut POWs!' came the awed whispers from all sides.

But the Big Nig wasn't impressed. He folded his black hands over his massive stomach and looked at them coldly. 'You can't fool the Big Nig, whitey,' he said icily. 'You're two Skorzeny goons, out to gun down the Supreme Commander. You're the guys who're gonna shoot Eisenhower. I figured it out as soon as Washington here contacted me. He's AWOL from the Triple A, which took part in the parade yesterday where there was an attempt on Ike's life. Funny, ain't it? Every white mouse in the whole of the goddam COMZ is looking for two white guys in connection with the attempted assassination – and you turn up; two middle-aged dudes who don't look like any Limey soldier the Big Nig's ever laid eyes on.'

Seadog was about to protest but just then the Count saw out of the corner of his eyes, with an awful sinking feeling, that Washington, their erstwhile partner, had drawn an ugly cut-throat razor from his pocket. He swallowed hard and uttered a silent prayer that the slim yellow soldier wouldn't use it on him where he feared he might . . .

But the Count was not fated to suffer that terrible death this day – though as a matter of fact he hadn't used *that* particular piece of his anatomy to any noticeable effect for many a long year. Instead, the Big Nig held up his black paw imperiously.

Hastily Washington slipped the cut-throat razor back into his pocket.

The Big Nig took his time before pronouncing his verdict, and even the Seadog, an unimaginative man at the best of times, felt the fear begin to well up sickeningly inside him.

'I know what you've come here to do. But,' he held up a forefinger the size of a black pudding, 'you tried to hit the wrong man yesterday.'

The Count's mouth dropped open stupidly, and Seadog gasped.

'*What* did you say?'

'The wrong man! That wasn't the real Ike – no, sir.' The Big Nig stared at them hard, all amusement gone from his gleaming face now. 'That guy was a double. You see, the Big Nig knows everything. He's got a better secret service than the US of A. Who sees niggers? They're invisible men, ain't they, brothers?' The bitterness was all too clear in his voice now.

There was a mutter of agreement from the other black soldiers, and the Count realized suddenly that the big Negro wasn't just talking to them, but to everyone in that low, crowded back room.

'We're everywhere, but we's niggers – and nobody pays no heed to niggers.' He stared hard at the Count and Seadog. 'So you want to kill the Su-preme Co-mmander, eh? Okay, the Big Nig knows where he is, and the Big Nig is gonna tell you how to do it. But this time for real. Now get a load of this, whiteys . . .'

Now it was almost dusk. Outside it was still snowing softly, and soon the orderlies would be coming in to put up the big black-out shutters. Yet still Bedell Smith worked hard at Eisenhower's raised desk at the far end of the big room, signing paper after paper in the name of his absent boss, while Major Cowen, laden with weapons and looking more like a one-man infantry division than ever, paced by the tall French windows.

Next to Otto, Charley sat slumped in his chair, bottle of beer in one hand, cigarette in the other, so immersed in his role as Supreme Commander that even the presence of the Chief of Staff didn't seem to intimidate him.

'You know, Otto, old buddy?' he said slowly. 'I kinda like being at the top of this power-pyramid thing. Here I am, pushing fifty, going a bit thin on top, putting on lard – and the broads fall over themselves to get between the sheets with me! Why, I ask you?'

Otto opened his mouth to answer, but Charley didn't give him a chance. 'Not on account of my good looks, Otto – no, sir!' He pointed the bottle of beer at the five stars on his shoulder. 'Because of those five bits of dime metal, that's why.' He laughed softly.

At the desk, Bedell Smith looked up and frowned severely, and Major Cowen ceased his clanking progress up and down by the windows, to hold his fingers up to his lips for silence. As he did so, Otto noticed he was now wearing a knuckle-duster.

'Funny, ain't it, Otto?' Charley continued, ignoring Cowen completely. 'As a second-looey, I have to slip Juicy Lucy – she's the big WAC who works in the typing pool, fourth desk from the right – a five each week just to give me a hand-job. *And* I have to bring my own baby oil! But as soon as I've got these five stars, I can have every babe in the joint – *for free*! I kid you not, Otto, those five stars have done wonders for my potency. Hell, at that party this afternoon, I was limping most of the time! If I'd gotten too close to a table, I'd have knocked the goddam bottles off it!'

Otto laughed softly. At least Charley wasn't so beer-serious as most of the Amis around Supreme Headquarters. With him, he could forget his worries about the future and the missing Count. 'Perhaps they'll let you play Eisenhower for Christmas, Charley.'

Charley's broad, mobile face lit up at the thought, and suddenly he looked more like Eisenhower than ever; he even seemed to have developed those extra Eisenhower teeth that he was always complaining he lacked.

'Gee, Otto, do you really think so? That *would* be swell! The best Christmas present I could ever get. *Ike for Christmas!*'

How little did they realize that afternoon how true Otto's prophesy would prove to be – and with what tragic results!

Five minutes later, it happened. As usual, Charley was required to act the part of the Supreme Commander returning to his private residence at the villa in St Germain. Strangely enough, only three months before, the same villa had been occupied by Field Marshal von Rundstedt, Supreme Commander of the German Forces in the West.

'Heaven, arse and cloudburst,' Otto had exploded when he'd learned who had been the previous occupant. 'You'd think those shits of generals would have better things to do than play musical chairs with each other! Now it's my turn, now it's yours!'

At the head of the 'General's' cavalcade rumbled a Sherman tank, its deck submerged by heavily-armed MPs laden with Tommy-guns; then came a jeep, also filled with policemen, and behind that Eisenhower's Packard, containing Bedell Smith, Otto, Major Cowen and naturally the 'Supreme Commander' himself. This in its turn was followed by more jeeps and another Sherman. Slowly the column rolled down the snow-filled drive of the Petit Trianon towards the road that led to St Germain, the guards lining the route saluting as the Packard passed, with Charley giving them full benefit of his face-splitting smile, in between surreptitious sips at his bourbon flask.

With the snow flying up on both sides of its whirling tracks, the leading Sherman ponderously manoeuvred itself onto the darkening road, the MP on patrol duty holding up all oncoming traffic to let it through. The first jeep followed, the MPs flashing suspicious glances to left and right. Then it was the Packard's turn, the driver cursing softly as the big saloon skidded on the new snow.

Gazing out of the car window, Bedell Smith noticed that, a little further up the road, a long six-wheeled Staghound armoured car, its engine ticking over softly, was waiting patiently for the convoy to pass. As they drew closer he saw that for some reason the canvas cap usually placed over its slim 37mm cannon when travelling had been removed. Instinctively Bedell Smith pulled out his little book and scribbled a note to be passed on by his staff to the outfit concerned, 'for disciplinary action'. After all, as the Chief of Staff always remarked when there were complaints, 'We can't *all* be nice guys like Ike. Somebody has to be a sonuvabitch around here, or the doughs wouldn't show respect, would they?'

He had just begun to write, 'at precisely sixteen hundred hours . . .', when it happened. The long, slim gun erupted.

Otto, looking through the rear window, saw the spurt of scarlet flame cut the grey evening gloom and the whole body of the Staghound tremble violently. Next moment, the Packard seemed to rear up in the air, as if it had life of its own, like a wild horse being put to the saddle for the first time.

In an instant, all was violent confusion. Otto felt himself hit the road hard. Charley slammed down on top of him, showering him with neat bourbon. Whistles shrilled. There was a blast of machine-gun fire. The traffic cop went down, his chest suddenly reduced to a mess of red. Cowen scrambled free of the smoking wreckage of the Packard and ran towards the Staghound, clumsily attempting to unsling his bazooka as he went, but forgetting that he was still wearing knuckledusters on both hands. With a grunt of surprise he suddenly pitched forward and fell face-down into the steaming shell-hole that had appeared as if by magic in his path. A policeman, showing great presence of mind that later gained him an instant commission – and a transfer to a combat unit where he was killed a month later – threw a smoke grenade at the Staghound. It exploded harmlessly in a thick white cloud of billowing smoke directly in front of the armoured car. But it did the trick: it prevented the unknown gunner from seeing his target, the 'Supreme Commander', who at that moment lay clasped in the arms of Otto Stahl, the pair of them looking like star-crossed lovers locked in a final embrace.

Now the sirens were howling everywhere in the Petit Trianon, and from all sides dark figures were running madly across the snowy courtyard to the scene of the ambush. The driver of the Staghound realized the danger. He rammed home reverse gear. The six-wheeled vehicle raced backwards down the road, followed by a hail of white-glowing tracer bullets which bounced off its steel sides like ping-pong balls to vanish into the grey gloom.

With a low whistle, Charley released Otto from his clutches and murmured in dazed awe, 'Christ on a crutch! Ike's bourbon sure has a helluva kick!'

DAY NINE: SATURDAY, DECEMBER 23rd, 1944

'When a good American dies, his soul goes to Paris.'

Old New England Saying

It was just after midnight, and it had stopped snowing at last, but the going was still treacherous – especially in the black-out. It wasn't surprising, therefore, that the black driver of the jeep took the slope leading to General Eisenower's hide-out carefully, grinding up the slick surface in second gear, his eyes fixed on the little patch of white track illuminated by his masked headlights. Finally he made it and came to a grateful halt in front of the guardhouse.

Four MPs surrounded the jeep, Tommy-guns at the ready, while a sergeant, hulking and broken-nosed, forty-five ready at his hip, flashed his torch at the jeep's two occupants: the skinny, yellow-faced driver at the wheel, and what looked like an elderly British officer in the rear, clutching a briefcase anxiously to his stomach.

'Could I have your ID, sir, please?' the NCO asked. The voice was polite enough, but his eyes were as suspicious as ever.

'Yes, of course, certainly,' the British officer answered, understandably nervous at the sight of the four armed policemen surrounding the jeep. He fumbled inside his greatcoat and brought out his pass, complete with photograph showing a fleshily handsome man with a somewhat dramatic cast of features, who looked more like an actor than a soldier.

'And may I ask what your business is here, sir?' asked the NCO.

'Naturally,' replied thc British officer, as if only too anxious to explain his presence here at this late hour.

'Courier from London. Urgent dispatches from Mr Churchill for General Eisenhower. Plane's arrival delayed at Orly. Damned snowstorm, you know. Have to wait till morning now to get my flight back. Damned nuisance!'

The NCO's face showed no expression, but inwardly he was amused. The Britisher spoke just as he had always expected the Limeys to speak. The elderly colonel could have been straight from a Hollywood 'B' movie.

'Okay,' said the NCO, 'report to the duty office, sir, please.' He flashed a glance at the green-glowing dial of his wrist-watch. 'It's exactly zero thirty hours now. I'll expect you to check out with me again at zero forty-five hours exactly.' He flashed the arrogant-looking black driver a quick look. He was obviously one of those lucky bastards working out of the drivers' pool at Orly Field, where they could pull all the French dames and live the life of Riley on the big black market smuggling racket currently flourishing between Paris and London. 'You got that, too, boy? Zero forty-five hours *exactly*!'

'Yassuh, Cap'n, I's got it!' the driver quavered, in the accents of the Deep South. 'Yas*suh*!'

The NCO slapped the hood of the jeep with his big hand. 'Okay, move it!'

The driver moved it.

Exactly fifteen minutes later, the same jeep came grinding down the slope towards the barrier again, its driver observing the 10 mph speed limit religiously. At the barrier, the driver once more halted the jeep, while the NCO flashed his torch inside. In the back, the British colonel, his briefcase still on his lap, was slumped as if fast asleep. The NCO nodded his approval. The driver released the brake and thrust home first gear, gunning his engine as if he were in a hurry.

The NCO grinned maliciously. 'Can't wait to get back to that Frog poon-tang at Orly, eh, boy?'

'No, suh,' the driver quailed, 'not me, suh. I's a law-abidin' boy, Cap'n, sir!'

'Then you just keep it that way, boy – 'cos where I come from, they string niggers up for just *thinkin'* them kind of things!'

The driver swallowed hard, eyes rolling wildly in the light of the torch. The NCO slapped the hood, and he let out the clutch too rapidly so that the jeep went coughing and bucking down the slope, leaving the NCO laughing in the drive behind it.

'Them nigras,' he proclaimed to no one in particular, 'sure do scare easily.' Then he turned and began to stamp back to the guardroom.

A hundred yards away, as the night swallowed up the lone jeep, Washington grinned at his own image reflected by the poor light in the windscreen.

'Damned stupid cracker!' he said contemptuously, and swung the wheel a little to the left to avoid a heap of snow which had fallen from the trees lining the road. 'What do *he* know?'

Behind him, dislodged by the sudden movement, the dummy in the uniform of the British Army tumbled slowly to the floor.

General Dwight D. Eisenhower couldn't sleep. He lay in the cramped little bedroom that had been allotted him to the front of the hide-out, smoking yet another Camel, spectacles thrust to the top of his balding head, *Hell-bent for Nevada* flung on the covers in front of him, half-read.

Outside, the wind blew softly, and he could tell by the change of temperature that there would be another fall of snow before daybreak. Now there was no sound, save the soft tramp of the sentries. He could almost have been the last man on earth.

The balding General who commanded the fate of nearly five million soldiers shivered. Once more he felt that three-o'clock-in-the-morning feeling which makes everything seem black and miserable. Of course, he knew that as soon as daylight came and the new day started, the feelings would vanish as if they had never been there – but daylight was hours away yet. How often had he experienced such feelings in these last years! And how much had happened in that time! From an obscure light colonel, he'd gone on to become the commander of the largest army that the United States had ever raised in its whole history: a man who might one day achieve the highest office in the land – *if* he played his cards right . . .

Eisenhower lit another Camel from the glowing butt held in his nicotine-stained fingers and wondered whether he should ring for an orderly to bring him a cup of Java. No – he decided against it. Who knows what might become of that orderly in years to come? One day he might be telling those bastard newspaper reporters that in the middle of the Kraut counter-offensive the boss couldn't sleep nights. That wouldn't look good when he was campaigning for president. He knew well that his future opponents would stoop pretty low in their mud-slinging campaign.

Eisenhower frowned at the ornate 18th century ceiling, with its plump cherubs blowing horns and nubile naked wenches, their tits seeming to be about to drop right into his upturned face. For some reason they made him think of Kay. What in Sam Hill's name was he going to do with her when the time came? They'd been together now since 1942, when she'd first been assigned to him as a driver by the Limey motor pool in Grosvenor Square. He'd gotten used to her in more ways than one. They'd had plenty of nice little hide-outs together – in Algiers, London and now in Paris. But when the war ended and the US Army, including himself, had to go back to the Zone of Interior,[1] what then? He could hardly see Mamie accepting Kay as his 'chauffeuse' back in Washington, and in that goddam gossip-shop *someone* was bound to get hold of what had been going on over in Europe sooner or later . . .

It was all very worrying. For a moment or two he

[1] US Army parlance for the United States

thought of the front and what might be happening there. But the problems there seemed so far away and unimportant in comparison with his personal ones that he dismissed the thought as quickly as it had come. The big problem was Kay.

He remembered the weekends they had spent together at Telegraph Cottage, just outside London. Had there been witnesses to those stolen hours? He thought of the odds and ends he'd given the red-haired 'chauffeuse': the four-leaf clover on paper with his initials, from Africa; the signed photos of them together in bathing dress in North Africa; the medals he'd gotten Churchill and Roosevelt to give her. What would the public make of all that, if they got to know? Could he trust his cronies – Butch, his public relations man; Tex, in charge of his office; Bedell 'Beetle' Smith, who might well have political ambitions of his own?

Slowly, as he tossed and turned in his big, lonely bed, hearing the wind rustle the snow-heavy trees outside, the Supreme Commander of the Allied Armies in Europe began to sweat.

'For Chrissake,' he moaned to the big stone wench with the dangling tits, *'what am I gonna do about Kay Summersby?'*

Not surprisingly, the baroque lady could give no answer to that question, but not far away, unknown to the tortured General, his problems were already being solved for him — drastically, violently, and for all time.

The Count shivered. His feet had turned to ice, and already the paralysing cold was beginning to creep up his legs to his stomach. He had never felt so cold in all his life, even in that terrible winter in war-torn Russia.[1] But in spite of his misery, the Count's brain was racing furiously.

Something terrible was going to happen tonight, he knew that instinctively. The Big Nig had dismissed him

[1] See *Otto and the Reds* for further details.

from the room before he had discussed the final details with Seadog, but Seadog's haggard, ashen face on emerging from that last discussion had told him all he needed. Clearly the huge black man was now hell-bent on revenge for all the indignities that he and his race had suffered at the hands of their white fellow-Americans.

Again, as he crouched there, huddled in a GI overcoat behind the shelter of what appeared to be a garden shed, the Count went over the details of his small role in the terrible proceedings to come. In essence, he guessed, he was to serve as a distraction. As soon as he heard the noise of the big truck coming up the long incline which led to the American General's hiding place, he was to do two things. 'It's very simple, Count,' Seadog had explained, speaking to him slowly and carefully, as if he were a backward child. 'You'll have two thermite grenades – quite harmless to human beings, by the way. One you'll throw towards the guard-post, the other towards General Eisenhower's house. Both will explode, giving off a bright, burning light, the intention being, according to you-know-who' – he lowered his voice and indicated the Big Nig, now busy with his own plotting behind them – 'to distract the guards and pinpoint the house.'

Instinctively, the Count also lowered his voice. 'But why get involved *now*, Seadog?' he objected. 'It's too late – and think of poor Otto. What –'

'Fuck poor Otto,' Seadog interrupted crudely. 'Let's think of our own hides, Count! If we don't go along with the Big Nig, he'll let that yellow bastard Washington loose on us with his cut-throat.'

The Count shuddered violently and grabbed his genitals protectively, as if Washington was already wielding that frightening blade of his.

'If we *do* go along with him, it means transportation back to the Reich. He's promised me on his mother's head that one of his Red Ball Express drivers will deliver us safely into German hands. Apparently he's worked out a deal with a small German unit dug in on a quiet front beyond Aachen to supply them with spam in return for cognac – spam's a drug on the French black market, you see,' he added, as if this was the most logical thing in the world.

'Oh, I see.'

'Besides,' Seadog pleaded cryptically, 'I'd dearly love to stick bananas up them before I get too old.' Suddenly he grabbed the Count's hand with an uncharacteristic show of emotion. 'Don't fail me, Count. Let the crazy nigger have his revenge any way he likes. But just let me do my thing with the bananas, *I beg you*!'

At the time, it had all been too much for the Count. Overwhelmed, all he had been able to stutter was, 'Well, all right, if you think it's so important.' But now as he crouched trembling in the freezing darkness of a December morning, Count von der Weide began to think again – seriously.

'You Otto Stahl?'

The harsh American voice suddenly broke into Otto's dream, and in an instant, a startled, naked Greta Garbo disappeared down the dark, misty corridor of fantasy, never to return.

Otto woke with a start.

A hard, white light blinded him. Instinctively he thrust out both hands to shield his eyes, and they fell on something soft, warm and delightfully yielding.

A woman gasped, and the harsh voice commanded. 'Okay, buddy, none of that. Freeze the mitts there!'

Otto did as he was ordered, and found himself to be holding a pair of woman's breasts, which he judged from long experience to be size 38, 'B' cup.

But he didn't stay holding them for long. For just then a horsey, well-bred English voice belonging to the owner of the aforementioned breasts addressed him.

'I say, will you please take your hands from my . . . er, *chest* and answer the question. Are you Otto Stahl?'

Reluctantly Otto removed his hands from the woman's 'chest' and, narrowing his eyes to slits against the blinding light, peered upwards. Leaning down over his cot was a pretty, green-eyed woman with bright red hair done up carefully in a white hair-net. Over her pyjamas of crêpe-de-chine, which revealed her figure pleasingly, she wore a GI greatcoat. On each side she was flanked by heavily armed, suspicious MPs.

'Yes, I'm Otto Stahl. Why? What's wrong?'

The bigger of the two bulls answered for the woman. 'Something very urgent has come up for a Second-Lieutenant Otto Stahl – that's you, ain't it?'

'Yes,' chimed in Kay Summersby, '— some person called the Count – though I must say, he doesn't sound like an *English* Count.'

'Count!' Otto exclaimed excitedly, cutting her short. 'Did you say Count?'

'Yes. He's on the phone right now, in the communications room downstairs. He asked to speak to me and said it was vitally urgent that I contacted you. Something to do with the Supreme Commander.'

'Yeah,' said the bigger of the two cops. 'You'd better move it, buster. *Now*!'

Hurriedly, Kay Summersby averted her eyes as Otto threw back the bedclothes. Rather to his embarrassment, Otto was still in a state of some excitement at the memory of those surprisingly pneumatic breasts.

The bigger cop gave a whistle of mock astonishment. 'Get a load of that, Al! I guess absence makes the horn grow hornier.'

His companion sniggered, and Otto said angrily, 'For Chrissake, give me my pants – quick!'

The moment Otto seized the phone in the blacked-out

communications room, he knew it was the Count all right. There was no mistaking that voice.

'Thank God, Otto . . . Thank God it's you, my boy. You can't imagine what trouble I'm in . . . I've just had to hit a fellow human being on the head so that I could use the phone. Oh, what a terrible thing! To use violence on the members of one's same species – '

'For God's sake, Count, shut up,' Otto bellowed, as the Count rambled on aimlessly, 'or I'll have to use violence on *your* member! Where are you? What are you up to, you silly old fart?'

Behind him, Kay Summersby and the two MPs exchanged startled glances as this supposed second-lieutenant of the US Army rattled on in fluent German. From outside in the corridor came the sound of running feet.

'I'm in the Supreme Commander's house, Otto, and I'm frozen and covered in pigeon droppings from the shed, and utterly miserable . . .'

'*Count*!' Otto exploded.

'You see the Big Nig told me about the Supreme Commander and the young lady, Miss Summersby, and I thought that if I could get through to her – oh dear, I only meant to tap the operator lightly on the head with the hammer, I didn't realize what brute strength I must possess – she'd pass on the warning.'

'*What warning*?' Otto screamed.

'That the Big Nig and Seadog and all those dark gentlemen are going to do something horrible to General Eisenhower!' Now the words came tumbling from the Count's mouth in an excited torrent. 'And I'm so afraid, I don't know which way to turn and, oh, Otto . . .*Help me*!'

Otto did a quick calculation, as the running feet came ever nearer. Just then, Major Cowen came gasping into view, laden with his full arsenal, now added to by a flak vest of the kind worn by bomber crews in the US Air

Force. Ignoring Otto, Cowen was busily stuffing a steel shaving mirror into his trousers to protect his genitals.

Otto switched his attention back to the Count. 'Now listen,' he rasped, 'Eisenhower will have his bedroom in the bottom of the house. You get to the highest point of the place – the attic, or somewhere like that. Understood?'

'Understood,' the Count quavered.

'Now get off that phone and get going. I'll take care of the rest. The highest point, remember – away from any possible danger. *Ende*!'

The phone went dead in Otto's hand in the same moment that a panting Bedell Smith pushed past Major Cowen, who was still fiddling with his flies, watched shyly by Miss Summersby.

'Now then, what's all this, Stahl?' barked Bedell Smith, while behind him, Cowen winced as the cold steel mirror came into contact with a sensitive part of his anatomy.

Hastily, Otto explained what the Count had told him.

Bedell Smith went pale. 'My God, so that attack yesterday was a goddam feint! I thought we parried it too darned easily. They were trying to lull us into a false sense of security while they set up Ike.' He clapped his hand to his forehead. 'It's ten miles to General Eisenhower's place – we'll never make it in this weather. Holy Cow, Cowen, don't just stand there playing with your ding-ding! *Do up your pants and sound the alarm!*'

The first flare came plunging down to earth, a glittering Christmas tree of sparkling flame, taking the convoy speeding towards Eisenhower's hiding-place by complete surprise.

Up front in the Packard, alongside Cowen, Otto, Kay Summersby and a snoring Charley, who had sunk back into a drunken sleep immediately after being bundled into the car, Bedell Smith groaned, 'Oh, no – not *that*! A fucking air raid – excuse my French, Kay!'

'Shall I stop the car, sir?' yelled the driver over the noise of the motor, as they raced down the narrow road. Now more and more of the big flares were starting to float out of the dark sky, turning night into day.

'No!' Bedell Smith cried urgently. 'The flak wagons will take care –'

Just then the rest of his words were drowned by the snarl of a high-speed engine, as a long, lean shape burst through the cloud of aluminium foil which was fluttering down from the sky like a swarm of sparkling exotic butterflies, to fool the American radar defences. Another shape followed. Two Messerschmitts, almost locked together, were barrelling down the road towards them at four hundred miles an hour, machine-guns crackling along the length of their wings, sending out angry, ugly blue spurts of flame.

Behind the Packard, the flak wagons – open scout cars with quadruple 20mm cannon mounted on their decks – took up the challenge. A stream of white tracer shells sped towards the planes.

Just when it seemed they were about to smash into the Packard, the two planes suddenly braked, swooping to left and right of the road to soar straight up into the burning sky, leaving behind them a wrecked, smoking jeep, its occupants sprawled on the rapidly melting snow in the grotesque postures of death.

'Across the fields, man!' Bedell Smith yelled, and wrenched at the big wheel. 'It's our only chance. No room to manoeuvre on this goddam Frog road!'

The driver closed his eyes and pressed his foot down hard on the accelerator. The car zoomed over the side and hit the snowy field beyond with a thud. Just in time. A burst of cannon-fire ripped up the road in the spot where they had just been, red flame spurting up as each shell exploded. Behind them a half-track, unable to brake in time, ran right into the shell-fire. Next instant its engine exploded, sending out a sheet of searing white flame.

Burning, screaming GIs tumbled out on all sides to writhe and wriggle in the snow, desperately trying to stifle the greedy, all-consuming flames.

Now they were bouncing and shaking across the field in a crazy zig-zag, throwing a wake of white snow six foot high behind them, followed by the surviving scout cars, their flak cannon still chattering furiously. Overhead, more and more flares came sailing down, turning the snow an eerie, unnatural hue.

Again the fighters came howling in for the kill. At ground level, they hurtled towards the vehicles, engines snarling ear-splittingly.

'Weave . . . For Chrissake, *weave*!' screeched Bedell Smith.

Frantically, his face glazed with sweat in the lurid reflected light of the flares, the driver spun the wheel left and right, throwing the heavy Packard into impossible turns and tossing its passengers like rag dolls from side to side – all save Charley, who snored on, happily oblivious to everything.

Now one of the Messerschmitts seemed to fill the whole world. It was roaring towards them on a collision course. Otto shut his eyes desperately. Cowen began to rattle off a prayer in Hebrew. Bedell Smith groaned, 'Oh, my God! And just when I get my third damned star!' Next to him, Kay Summersby pulled hard at her too-short khaki skirt. Even at this critical moment she didn't want anyone to see that she was wearing issue knickers with elastic at the knees.

Closer and closer the Messerschmitt came in. Now the pilot was lowering his undercarriage and lifting up the plane's nose. Bedell Smith knew why. By doing this, the pilot could reduce the speed of the plane. This time he couldn't miss!

Behind Bedell Smith, Otto gazed at the plane in horror. He could make out every detail of it, right down to the rivets on the fuselage and the white blur of the pilot's face as he came in for the kill. '*Gott im Himmel,*' he cried, appalled at the injustice of it all. To be killed by one of his own people, in the middle of nowhere! He tensed and waited like a dumb animal for the inevitable slaughter.

But it was not to be. Behind Otto, the stricken half-track suddenly exploded in a great, thick white cloud of smoke and flame. Tracer zig-zagged crazily into the burning sky. Huge pieces of metal howled overhead, peppering the air like flak. Suddenly, with a blinding roar, the hovering fighter took a hit. One moment it was there, the next it was exploding into a thousand pieces. Otto gasped. A strange, crouched shape was hurtling through the air towards them. At a tremendous speed, it slammed right against the bonnet of the Packard. The car came to an abrupt halt, its nose crumpled like a squashed banana. Slowly, very slowly, what was left of the pilot dropped to the snow, as the steam hissed furiously from the ruptured radiator – the only sound in that sudden reverberating silence . . .

'Easy as falling off a goddam log,' said the Big Nig easily, as the two trucks, canvas hoods tightly tied down at the back to conceal the men inside, bowled along the dead-straight French road, the pines flashing by on both sides in a blur of ghostly green. He puffed at his big cigar, his fat black face wreathed in a happy smile, as if he hadn't a care in the world.

Seadog frowned. He wondered just how far he could trust the big black man. He made it all seem so easy. Yet his experience told him that there had to be a catch in it somewhere – and for him. Why should the man sitting next to him, who hated white men with a passion, help *him*? It stood to reason: the Big Nig was out to double-cross him. The question was: *how?*

Just then, Seadog happened to glance in the rearview mirror. Through the crack in the ragged canvas to the rear of the cab, he caught a glimpse of a familiar grey uniform – the field-grey of the German Wehrmacht – with above it a coal-black face under a heavy coal-scuttle helmet. He bit his bottom lip as they drove on, while next to him, the Big Nig happily hummed a Negro spiritual.

Everything was beginning to fall into place. Fanatic though he was, the Big Nig wasn't going to risk his future by committing a crime that would set the whole of the US Army's police *apparat* searching for him, Seadog reasoned. Instead, he was going to use the Skorzeny business to cover up. Why else would his men wear German uniforms? The question was, what role did he envisage for the only two white men – Germans, to boot – in this operation? As things stood, the Count was going to pinpoint the target and the guard-house. He was to help storm the house. But the Big Nig already knew every detail of Eisenhower's hide-out, from his black secret service of the Red Ball Express. What help could two middle-aged men, one of them hampered by a peg-leg, be to these fit young blacks, half their age? Furthermore, the Big Nig had already told him that he wouldn't be taking part in the operation himself. 'Too much blubber,' he had explained, prodding his massive gut and lifting his shirt to reveal the thick folds of fat. 'Probably have a goddam heart-attack if I ran more than six steps!' He had chuckled merrily, 'Save my physical activity for a roll in the hay with the Frog whores. If I'm gonna kick off, I reckon there's no better place than on the job, eh, Kraut!' And he had nudged Seadog knowingly. Thinking back to that moment now, the German remembered there had been no humour in the Big Nig's dark, cunning little eyes.

Once more Seadog bit his lip anxiously. They were being set up – him and that stupid old aristocrat, Comte de la Prairie, as he insisted on calling himself when introduced to the niggers' French whores. They wouldn't survive this operation. They were going to be killed and their bodies left behind as evidence – evidence that the men who had murdered the Supreme Commander belonged to one of Skorzeny's goon squads.

As he sat there next to the massive bulk of the Big Nig, now cheerfully humming 'All God's chillun', Seadog felt an icy finger of fear trace its way down his spine. They were going to be murdered – and he'd never get to stick bananas up nubile black maidens. He had to *do* something. *He had to*!

The trucks rolled on.

The Count awoke with a start. Suddenly his nostrils were assailed by the stink of pigeon droppings and the dust of centuries. He blinked his eyes and peered around in the grey gloom of the attic, wondering for a moment where he was. Then he remembered. He had followed Otto's advice, and after thrusting a soft cushion under the unconscious telephone operator's head with a muttered 'Sorry' and scribbling a hasty 'get-well-soon' note on his message pad, he had searched the rambling 18th-century house until he had found the attic. There, despite the freezing cold, he must have dropped off almost straight away, thermite grenades clutched defensively in both hands.

Now he placed them gingerly on the bare, dusty floorboards and looked at the green-glowing dial of his watch. '*Il est cinq heures*,' he said to himself in French – for in his new role of Comte de la Prairie he always spoke French. '*C'est l'heure zéro*.'

The Count walked to the sloping skylight and eased it open. The snow slithered from it in a miniature avalanche, and the Count peered out, shivering as the dawn cold struck his sleep-heavy face.

It was snowing softly again, but in spite of the weather, the guards posted at the gate seemed vigilant enough. In the grey, whirling gloom he could just make out the machine-gunners crouched over their weapon in the sand-bagged enclosure at the gate, and to their front, the MP at the barrier-pole, huddled in his greatcoat, bayoneted rifle slung over his shoulder.

The Count craned his neck to the right. There he could just distinguish the snow-covered shape of a Sherman tank, slowly disappearing from sight in the gloom. It seemed empty, but the Count could tell from the thin wisps of blue cigarette smoke emerging from its turret that it, too, was manned. Eisenhower was well protected all right, but were his guards prepared for a surprise attack of the kind the Big Nig had planned?

Again the Count looked anxiously at his watch. '*Où sont ils*?' he asked aloud, wiping a spot of fresh pigeon shit from the dial. By now Otto should have alerted a rescue party and be approaching the villa. If he hadn't, the worst would happen . . .

He licked his parched lips and stared hard at the small, winding country road, flanked on both sides by spiked firs, which led up to the remote French country house, combing the landscape for the first sign of headlights, which would signify rescue and an end to this whole mad business.

Suddenly he started, his weariness completely forgotten. A pair of dimmed headlights had just appeared around the bend in the road. He breathed a sigh of relief.'*Ils sont là!*' he whispered to himself. '*Les braves gars – ils sont là!*'

Otto had arrived just in time.

As the first truck came gently to halt to wait for the Count's signal, the Big Nig was suddenly struck by a memory. The day after they had arrived in France, they had been addressed by old Blood an' Guts Patton himself. Mistaking the new arrivals for a combat battalion, he had given them one of his red-hot fighting speeches, full of vigorous profanity and bloodthirsty sentiments. Standing up there on the rostrum, famous pistols on his hips, gleaming lacquered helmet on his head and wearing an immaculate tailored uniform, he had told his black listeners in that high-pitched squeaky voice of his, 'Men, you are the first Negro unit to fight in the American Army in Europe. I would never have asked for you if you were not good. I'll have nothing but the best in my army. I don't care what colour you are as long as you go up there and kill those Kraut sons-of-bitches! Everyone has their eyes on you and is expecting great things from you. Most of all, your race is looking forward to your success. Don't let them down, and damn you, don't let *me* down!' Patton paused, glaring around their sweaty black faces, then declared, 'If you want me, you can always find me with the lead element. They say it is patriotic to die for your country. *Well, let's see how many patriots we can make of those Kraut motherfuckers!'*

They had cheered themselves, hoarse, throwing their caps into the air, carried away by an overwhelming feeling of patriotism, of belonging to a common cause, all past ill-treatment and resentment forgotten. At that moment the Big Nig had decided to forget his ideas of deserting, and instead do all he could to bring about a victory for the Allied cause.

Twenty-four hours later he had been dancing a jig in a Frog bar, sweating with fear, lumbering around like a black hippo, while drunken redneck crackers from the 29th Infantry made matchwood of the floor with their forty-fives all around his flying feet. Exactly three hours later he had sold the truck he had been driving and its contents to a greasy little Frog crook – and gone over the hill.

As he sat there now in the cooling cab of the truck, waiting, listening to the rustle of the snowflakes on the hood and the soft whispers of the men in the back, the Big Nig remembered that summer, and felt his heart harden and that old, old burning rage overcome him once more. They'd pay, the whiteys. Hot shit, how they'd pay for the centuries of injustice and ill-treatment! Now, in 1944, the Krauts would be credited with the slaying of the USA's top soldier, Eisenhower; but one day when his people were finally free – and free they would be – *then* he'd let the world know who had really killed the 'Su'preme Co'mmander'. A black man! One of the so-called 'invisible men'!

Half a mile away, the Count decided to act. Why was Otto waiting out there? If he didn't come soon, that coarse one-legged sailor and his repulsive black companion would beat them to it. He *had* to attract their attention. Besides, he badly needed to urinate, and there seemed to be no toilet facilities in the attic. He took up one of the thermite grenades, and remembering Seadog's instructions, pulled the pin. Almost immediately the long tube started to hiss and fizz alarmingly, little white sparks beginning to splutter from the top.

'*Mon Dieu!*' gasped the Count, and hastily thrust the skylight open even wider. The thing was buzzing away frighteningly now. Sparks were raining everywhere. Panicked beyond measure, the Count tossed the grenade blindly into the whirling snow, so that it landed directly on the turret of the Sherman below.

Suddenly everything happened at once. A whistle shrilled. Someone yelled '*Fire!*' Another hoarse voice cried, '*It's Skorzeny and the whole of the Kraut army!*' The tank's engine burst into life with an ear-splitting roar and the Sherman lurched forward, 75mm cannon already pounding, straight into the glasshouse opposite, grinding to a stop in a rain of glass.

In an instant all was curses, cries, chaos. Sirens wailed. Someone screamed '*Air raid! Air raid!*' A man came running out into the snow, twirling a gas rattlemask already in place. An early-morning cook followed, hobbling along with one foot stuck inside a can of pancake mix, and clutching at his throat dramatically, gasping as he sank to his knees in the snow, 'I can't breathe . . . *Can't breathe . . .*'

Up on the height, the Big Nig was suddenly galvanized into action.

'Take her away, Washington!' he yelled, dropping neatly out of the cab as Washington rammed home first gear. In the back of the truck, the black soldiers dressed in the field-grey of the Wehrmacht began to call out, as ordered, '*Sieg Heil! Fuck de Amerikaner Führer Eisenhower . . . Sieg Heil!*' With a lurch, the truck jolted forward, while down below the searchlights flicked on and started sweeping the snowy fields for the first signs of the attackers.

Seadog, white and quaking with terror and knowing now that he was heading straight for his death, hung on for all he was worth as the truck thundered towards the gate. What the hell could he do?

Suddenly the machine-gun posted at the gate started to spit fire at the first truck. Tracer cut through the air, gathering speed by the instant, hurtling straight at them like lethal white rain.

'Holy shit!' Washington gasped. 'What's this? I'm coloured . . . They ain't supposed to fire at me, the motherfuckers! This ain't no coloured boy's war, goddamit!'

Madly he wrenched the wheel to one side to avoid the hail of slugs. The cab door flew open. Suddenly Seadog felt himself falling. In vain he tried to grab hold. '*Help!*' he screamed, and went flying out. His peg-leg hit something hard and splintered like matchwood. Next moment he was squatting on the ground with the remains of his wooden leg poking in an extremely sensitive place. Seadog gave a moan of pain. Suddenly he seemed to have lost all desire to poke bananas up nubile young ladies.

It hurt like hell!

'Trouble! There's trouble ahead!' Otto yelled above the clatter of the Packard which was now running on a flat tyre and bumping clumsily up and down on the road. '*Look!*'

He pointed through the snow, to where tracer could be seen, whizzing through the grey gloom. Red flames flickered, and the boom of a tank cannon rang out, muffled by the falling snow.

'Oh, my God!' gasped Bedell Smith. 'It's Ike! They've bushwhacked him – and he hasn't even had a chance to get his fifth star from that bastard in the White House! Driver, give it all you've got!'

'I'm a non-combatant,' Charley yelled, waking out of a drunken sleep, 'and well over age, too!' In the back of the Packard, Kay Summersby pulled at her skirt. Major Cowen straightened his flak vest. 'There are no better scrappers in the US Army than us New York Irish-Americans,' he proclaimed proudly, putting on his 'Jimmy Cagney' face. Otto groaned and covered his eyes with his hands.

Like the Seventh Cavalry galloping to save a beleagured wagon train, the battle-scarred Packard belted down the road, followed by the survivors of the surprise air attack – a bedraggled convoy gallantly charging to the sound of the guns . . .

'*Holy cow!*' gasped an MP. 'The Krauts are using *their* niggers!'

'Well, I'll shit in my hat!' called another.

Both men watched open-mouthed as the first truck began discharging its cargo of grey-clad black soldiers.

'Thank God we've got the Klu Klux Klan. At least our negros know their place,' cried the machine-gunner, too stupefied by the sight of the black faces under those familiar coal-scuttle helmets even to press the trigger of his machine-gun. 'They wouldn't *dare* to pull a lulu like —' Just at that moment a grenade sailed through the air. Someone fired a wild burst — and missed. Wood and brick splinters flew everywhere. Suddenly the black Wehrmacht was surging forward through the gate, screaming '*Sieg Heil!*' hysterically.

In the shattered glasshouse, the turret of the Sherman hissed round. Its long 75mm cannon spurted flame. The first shell howled over the heads of the running black soldiers. Here and there a man skidded to a stop, halted in his tracks by the tremendous wave of blast. With a thick, angry *crump*, the HE shell exploded. Fist-sized shards of red-hot metal sliced through the air. Men went down screaming shrilly on all sides, attackers and defenders both. Up in his hiding place, watching the crazy scene below as if mesmerized, the Count gasped with horror as a coal-black head complete with helmet sailed level with his window and seemed to stay there for an age, grinning wide-eyed, before plummeting to earth once more.

Otto's Packard slammed into the mangled wreckage of the gate. The passengers tumbled out in a crazy heap. Cowen tried to run forward, but the strap of his bazooka caught round his knees and he fell flat on his face in the snow, closely followed by Charley, who was whimpering abjectly, '*I surrender! I surrender!*' Kay Summersby tugged her khaki blouse straight, surveyed the shambles all around, and said in her most British voice, 'I say, who's in charge here?' but understandably, none of the moaning, wounded MPs was in a position to answer her.

Bedell Smith, his face flushed and angry, pulled out his forty-five. 'Come on!' he barked above the snap and crackle of small arms fire to their front, as the black Wehrmacht raced ever closer to the Supreme Commander's hide-out. 'We've got to save Ike before it's too late! They're —' The rest of his words were drowned by the thunder of the tank's gun, as another huge hundred-pound shell tore the grey dawn apart.

Together, he and Otto pelted towards the house, zig-zagging crazily like football players making an end run. A burst of automatic fire kicked up the snow at their feet. Bedell Smith swerved to the right to avoid it. The line of slugs raced towards Otto. He swerved violently to the left. Suddenly a black soldier dressed in field-grey sprang out of the outhouse in front of him. '*Amerikaner kaputt!*' he cried hysterically, and charged Otto with his bayonet fixed. Otto reacted instinctively. He halted and as soon as his attacker was close enough, kicked up and under the levelled rifle. The black screamed shrilly and went reeling backwards, rifle tumbling to the snow as he grabbed for his ruined testicles. Hardly pausing, Otto grabbed the rifle and ran on.

A grenade sailed through the air from one of the villa's smashed windows. Otto dived hard for the snow. It flew overhead and disappeared into the grey gloom. Next moment, its explosion was drowned as the panicked crew of the Sherman fired again, and another HE shell erupted against the nearest wall in a sheet of ugly red flame. A hail of slates and bricks showered down, the smoke clearing to reveal a huge tear in the side of the building. '*God Almighty*,' Otto cursed wildly, 'they're gonna kill Ike themselves if they're not careful!' Madly he scrambled to his feet and ran on. He had to find the Count before it was too late.

A door was flung open. A fat man in a dirty white cook's apron stumbled out, cleaver raised, ready to do battle, mumbling to himself in a language Otto took to be Italian. 'Friend!' Otto gasped, as the cook raised his hatchet. 'I'm a—'

Next moment the hatchet came hissing down, the cook's dark eyes blazing with rage.

Otto hopped back hurriedly. 'Hey, knock it off!'

The cook swung the hatchet again. Otto ducked. Now he'd had enough. He rammed home the brass-shod butt of the rifle. The cook howled, his eyes going crossed as the butt connected with his swarthy, unshaven chin. He fell, as if pole-axed. Otto sprang over his body.

An officer stepped out of a side door. His fist lashed out. Otto yelped with pain and dropped his rifle. The punch sent him reeling back, a trickle of blood emerging from his nostril like a timid animal venturing out at first light from its burrow.

'*Dreckschwein!*' Otto cursed, and sprang back to the attack. But before he could close with the officer, there was a huge, ear-splitting explosion. It whipped Otto against the opposite wall, and for what seemed like an age, he was pinned there, gasping for breath helplessly like an asthmatic in the throes of an attack. Outside he could hear a furious Bedell Smith shouting, 'For God's sake, Cowen, stop that crazy tank gunner! He's gonna kill the goddam lot of us!' Opposite Otto, the officer who had attacked him was beginning to sink from view into an enormous hole which had appeared suddenly in the middle of the floor, terrified, meaningless sounds bubbling from his ashen lips. Then he was gone, and Otto raced on.

Somehow in the smoke and the confusion, he found the stairs. A man lay sprawled across them, bottle clutched to his chest. Whether he was dead or drunk, Otto didn't know or care. His first concern was to find the Count and get out of this crazy Ami house before it was too late. He pelted up the steps. Again, the Sherman's cannon thundered. The whole house reeled as if struck by a violent storm, and dimly Otto heard Bedell Smith bellow 'Use your goddam bazooka on the bastard, Cowen!' Angry blue flames flared on all sides and his nostrils were assailed by the first smoke of the inferno to come. Blindly he reeled on, the cries and calls for help growing ever fainter behind him.

For a long time, or so it seemed, he blundered about, ripping open door after door in his search for the Count. At one point a boot came flying his way and a soldier yelled 'Fuck off, Sarge – just let me sleep!' as Otto ran on, he noticed smoke already beginning to curl around the sleeper's bed like a silent grey cat. At last he saw him – that familiar figure with his fleshy face and dramatic eyes, standing in the hallway, hands extended theatrically, as if he were Dr Livingstone about to greet Mr Stanley in the middle of the Dark Continent – though the pigeon shit which covered his steel helmet rather destroyed the illusion.

'*Mon cher Otto* –' began the Count, but Otto, gasping for breath, cut him short with an angry, 'Shut up, you silly old fart! Let's get out of here before it's too late!' He turned, grabbing the Count's hand, as if to drag him off like a recalcitrant child.

Then it happened.

There was a huge bang, and Otto felt his feet swept from beneath him by a great howling wind. His lungs felt about to burst. Noises like the boom of great bells assailed his ears. Silver and red stars exploded in front of his eyes. From somewhere a black mist began creeping over him. '*Otto! OTTO!*' came the Count's voice, as if from a long, long way away. And slowly but inexorably, Otto started to sink to the heaving, bucking floor, as all around him, the world came tumbling down . . .

DAY TEN: SUNDAY, DECEMBER 24th, 1944

'God rest ye, merry gentlemen, let nothing ye dismay.'

Traditional Christmas Carol

In latter years it was generally recognized that Christmas Eve, 1944, marked the turning-point in the great German counter-offensive in the Ardennes. For the very first time since the surprise attack had started, there was no fog or overcast. Instead, the sky was hard, brilliant, blue: ideal weather for flying. The American Air Force, grounded since December 16th, didn't wait for a second invitation. From dawn to dusk, their planes were in the air in their thousands, pounding the German columns driving for the Meuse. Already, too, Patton's attack on the left flank of the German armies was beginning to make itself felt, especially now that his tankers of the Third Army were getting the support of seven groups of fighter-bombers, eleven groups of medium bombers, a division of the 8th US Air Force and a smattering of RAF planes.

That day, not surprisingly, Germany's senior commander in the Ardennes, diminutive ex-gentleman-jockey, General von Manteuffel, called the Führer's HQ and informed Hitler's Chief of Staff that in essence, the great attack in the west couldn't succeed and was already running out of steam. Instead of attempting to cross the Meuse, von Manteuffel suggested, 'I'll wheel north on *this* side of the Meuse, and we'll trap all the Allies on the east of the river.'

However, this limited solution wasn't accepted, and so Germany's defeat in the west was virtually sealed.

But the question that has long puzzled students of what has since been called 'America's European Pearl Harbor' is *where* were the Allied senior commanders on December

24th, 1944, the day that brought the end of Germany's hopes in the west?

It has been long assumed that they were at the front, or at least in their forward command posts, just behind the firing line. Yet all records are decidedly vague as to their whereabouts on that beautiful winter's day when victory was in the air. Naturally, during the war, all details of senior generals' activities were kept secret; to reveal them could have helped the enemy. Yet even forty years later, long after the strange and complicated events of that day, little is know of what Generals Montgomery, Patton, Bradley and Eisenhower did that particular Sunday.

The official diaries are completely blank, save for a few vague phrases, with no times or places indicated. All we know of those four generals' whereabouts is what we can glean from members of their official households, few of whom were in a position to know what was *really* going on.

General Patton's movements on the 24th are recorded in the diary of his aide, Colonel Charley Codman, who states that his boss was at the front most of the day in a jeep, alone save for his driver Sergeant Mims, appearing much later to boost civilian morale in Luxembourg by attending 'Christmas Eve services at the Protestant Church in the centre of the city, occupying the pew formerly reserved for the Kaiser.'

Possibly, General Bradley went with him, but if so, Bradley himself makes no mention of the fact in his own account of those days. His first mention of that Christmas Eve is when he records that he received a telephone call from Montgomery asking him to visit him on the 25th, and describes the complicated arrangements made to fly him to Monty's HQ in his plane, the *Mary Q*. As for Monty, the only officer who might know, Major John Poston, the 'Master's' closest disciple, has been dead, killed in action, these forty years.

All we know of Eisenhower's movements, despite the fact that his headquarters was enormous, consisting of

5,000 military and civilian personnel, is a brief reference in Kay Summersby's book on her former boss; in it she states that in spite of the continuing threat to Eisenhower's life from Skorzeny's goon squads, Ike grumbled, 'Hell's fire, I'm going out for a walk. If anyone wants to shoot me, he can go right ahead. I've got to get out!'

A strange desire, when one considers that General Eisenhower was in considerable pain from a renewed injury, suffered in a plane crash, to his 'trick knee', which had almost caused him to be fired from West Point as a 'plebe'. *Yet Ike wanted to walk*!

So where *were* the top generals that Christmas Eve, and why were their movements kept secret ever afterwards? Otto Stahl thought he knew then. Today, he is absolutely *sure* that on that Sunday, he and the Count were witness to one of the most amazing cover-ups in the whole of history . . .

They were all there. There was no mistaking them as they gathered down below in the snowy courtyard of the Versailles HQ, waiting for the staff cars to carry them back to their own headquarters. Monty – small, sloppy and sway-backed, balanced on a rusty green gamp; Bradley – bespectacled and lantern-jawed, looking like a country school-teacher in uniform; Patton – towering over the rest, as immaculate as ever, fingering his ivory-handled pistols, as if he might be tempted to use them at any moment; Ike – standing slightly to one side in front of Bedell Smith and Kay Summersby; and Major Cowen, grinning as always, yet without conviction . . .

Supported by the Count, a pale-faced Otto, his head swathed in thick bandages and aching like hell from the explosion, peered down at the Top Brass of the Allied armies, wondering what they were doing here.

'Something to do with Christmas Eve, d'you think, Count?' he ventured, as the first old-fashioned Rolls Royce bearing the standard of Field Marshal Montgomery began to nose its way into the courtyard. 'The Amis really do love to give parties, even when there's a war on.'

The Count frowned. 'Don't know Otto,' he said *sotto voce*, in case anyone might be listening to them, up here on the third floor of the Petit Trianon. 'Some funny things have been going on here since the explosion knocked you out.'

'What sort of things, Count?' Otto asked without interest, his eyes remaining glued to the group below. Now Bedell Smith seemed to be talking heatedly to the assembled Brass, a couple of times gesturing upwards.

'Well, for a start, all the black men have vanished – at least, the ones who got inside the house. The crew of that Sherman that was doing all the wild shooting have disappeared as well.' The Count snapped his fingers. 'Vanished into thin air!'

'Perhaps they put them in jail. The shits deserved it.'

'No, Otto. Seadog and the – er, Big Nig – they've both been captured by the US authorities. They're in the stockade, as your Major Cowen calls it.'

Down below, Bedell Smith seemed to be in earnest conversation with Cowen, ignoring Ike, and a couple of time pointing upwards.

'So where did they go?' asked Otto.

The Count shrugged a little helplessly. 'I don't really know, Otto, but I *do* know that there's a sentry outside the door of this room, armed with a rifle. Whether he's there to keep us in or to keep someone else out, I can't tell you, my dear boy.'

Otto frowned painfully. 'But why? We helped to save the Supreme Commander's life! What danger can we possibly present now – especially as Seadog is the last of the Skorzeny group and as you say, he's in the bag, quite harmless?'

But before the Count had time to answer, Patton's gleaming staff car rolled into the courtyard, twin klaxons howling, hemmed in on both sides by two score outriders, all armed with grease-guns and looking as if they might use them at the slightest provocation.

Now the Brass's party started to break up rapidly; clearly each senior commander was eager to be on his way. Salutes were exchanged, drivers gunned their engines, doors were opened and slammed, ribald or seasonal greetings were exchanged – and then they were gone, speeding out of the courtyard, leaving Ike, Kay and Bedell Smith waving farewells, while Ike's black terrier, Scottie, barked and frolicked madly at their heels.

It was then, and only then, that Otto noticed that the Supreme Commander had a small bottle of French beer sticking out of the back pocket of his khaki pants. With a gasp of astonishment, he realized that the man waving goodbye to the brass wasn't General Eisenhower at all – *but Second-Lieutenant Charley Chatham, the one-time pride of the summer stock theatre* . . .

Five minutes later there was a hearty knock on the door of their room and without waiting to be asked in, a surprisingly sprightly Major Cowen burst in, minus the arsenal of the previous days, but now bearing the silver insignia of a light colonel at his throat.

'Hello, old buddy!' he said, slapping Otto on the arm. 'Bright-eyed and bushy-tailed again, I see, Otto! Fine, fine . . .' Cowen beamed, yet Otto noted that for some reason, he avoided looking directly at the two men. *Why*? 'What about you folks coming out with me in the jeep for a ride? It's a beautiful winter's day. Do your poor old head a world of good. Besides,' he winked hugely, 'I just happen to know a cute old Frog *estaminet*, where it's an "on" day.[1] I guess it wouldn't hurt none to celebrate my promotion now, would it?'

[1] During the war, alternate days in France were 'non-alcoholic' *i.e.* bars served no alcohol – officially.

Immediately, the Count forgot his uneasy fears, and Otto found himself being hurried into his greatcoat. The newly promoted light colonel talked all the time, as if he hardly dared allow a moment's pause in the conversation; yet all the while Otto had a sensation that something was wrong . . .

'How's old Charley getting on?' he ventured carefully, as Cowen ushered them down the corridor.

'Great . . . Great, Otto,' Cowen answered hastily. 'Gone back to his outfit. Don't need him now that we've dealt with Skorzeny's goon squad – thanks to you gentlemen. Yeah, old Charley's been busted back to second looey again.' He held out his hand like a waiter ushering honoured guests to the best part of the restaurant. 'This way, gentlemen.'

Otto frowned. Cowen was lying. *Why*?

They set out in an open jeep. Behind them at a discreet distance another jeep followed, containing three armed MPs, whose presence Cowen dismissed with an airy wave of his hand. 'Now I'm a light colonel, I get a couple of Joes riding shotgun for me – nothing to worry about, Otto!'

Slowly Cowen eased the jeep out of the headquarters, where already little Christmas trees were beginning to be set up at the tall French windows, with bespectacled office workers fussing over them and arranging presents and candles as if they were back in some American middle-class suburb.

'Beautiful day, ain't it?' Cowen remarked casually, 'The trees are cute, too. Always go to church on Christmas Eve back home, but I'll skip it today for your sake.'

The road glittered like polished steel in the hard winter sunshine. The sky was a perfect deep blue, combed here and there by the brilliant white contrails of the Fortresses, flying east to pound the enemy. The dark green of the pines merged into one long, beautiful sweep. The air was like wine. In all, it was a perfect Christmas Eve day, the kind Otto seemed to remember from his youth . . . In those days it always used to snow the night before Christmas Eve, and the next day they would all stand in front of the gleaming, candle-bright Christmas tree, reciting their Christmas poem before they received their presents,[1] and gazing out at the sun sparkling on the perfect white of the snow outside the '*gute Stube*'[2] of his grandparents' house . . .

But today the beauty of his surroundings was lost on Otto; he was too puzzled – and not a little scared. What was going on? What had happened to the blacks? Where was the real Eisenhower? Why was Cowen taking them out for a ride like this, with a bodyguard of armed white mice? *And why had he lied about Charley*?

He cast a sideways glance at Cowen at the wheel, but his dark, skinny face revealed nothing. As he drove, the newly promoted light colonel was happily singing, '*I've got spurs that jingle-jangle-jingle, as I go riding merrily along*,' in a fair imitation of the Old Groaner. At that moment he appeared not to have a care in the world. Yet twice in the last five minutes he had shot a glance at the rear-view mirror, obviously checking whether the escort was still there.

Suddenly Otto had an inspiration. He turned to the Count next to him.

'Listen, arse-with-ears,' he said in his thickest Berlin accent, so that Cowen couldn't listen in, 'out with the language. What happened yesterday? Did you see the big animal at all?' He meant Eisenhower.

The Count was still bewildered at Otto's sudden acquisition of a thick working-class Berlin-Wedding dialect, but he reacted with surprising speed for him.

While Cowen stopped singing and listened acutely, the Count answered, 'The metal monster fired again after you got hit on the turnip and went out. The shell hit the room beneath us, and both of us were blown outside – er, arse

[1] Presents are given out on Christmas Eve afternoon in Germany.

[2] The 'best room'.

over tip.' He paused, his cheeks flushed slightly red with pride at his success with the unfamiliar *argot*.

Otto sucked his bottom lip thoughtfully. 'So the nigs that took part in the bust-up vanished as well as the *real* big animal,' he mused aloud. 'So only you and Mrs Stahl's handsome son know that the big animal has a double – and that the double was playing the big animal in the courtyard back –'

Suddenly the jeep braked. A bell jingled. Ahead of them, a red-and-white barrier pole with a shaking curtain of wires started to descend. A level crossing. Slowly a heavily-laden troop train started to chug across the track in front of them, smokestack belching fumes and sparks like a volcano. Most of the war-shattered windows of the ancient coaches had been boarded up and only a slit left for vision, but here and there, there was still glass in the compartment windows, and through it Otto had a glimpse of pale, scared young faces: the faces of cannonfodder being sent to the front to end their short lives brutishly and terribly. But he also saw something else. Mirrored in the glass was the image of the MPs in the vehicle parked immediately behind them, their faces set and intent beneath their heavy white helmets, their eyes blazing as if they were angry and spoiling for a fight.

Otto shuddered.

'Louse run over your liver, eh, Otto?' The Count queried pleasantly, waving half-heartedly to the young soldiers, who didn't wave back.

'Yes,' Otto said. 'With hob-nailed ammunition boots.'

The French locomotive gave a whoop like an Indian war-cry. A burst of steam. The wheels started to move more rapidly, and then the troop train was past, two red tail-lights disappearing into the distance. Slowly the barrier creaked upwards and the jeep jolted forward over the sleepers. And at that precise moment, Otto, realized with a shiver of pure terror that *they knew too much*.

They knew that the real Eisenhower was dead. They

knew that the Top Brass this morning had planned a great deception. Perhaps their aim was to keep the alliance together; perhaps to fool the Germans in this vital stage of the Allied campaign in Europe – the reasons didn't matter. What *did* matter was that they, Otto Stahl and Count von der Weide, knew about Charley and knew what had happened at that remote hide-out last night, and . . . Otto gulped hard and felt his throat flood with hot, sickening bile. Harshly he forced himself to think his thought to its final, terrible conclusion. *And they were going to kill them because of it . . . Kill them dead this very morning*!

'But they couldn't – er, croak us on Christmas Eve,' the Count hissed in protest, as the jeep began to slow down. 'Not on Christmas Eve!'

'Silly old fart,' Otto growled. 'They're killing each other by the thousand at the front. Why should we be any different? *Not on Christmas Eve!*' He gave a snort of exasperation.

'Anything wrong?' Cowen asked, easing the jeep into what appeared to be an abandoned quarry next to the road, which was now, Otto noted with alarm, completely deserted.

'What should be wrong?' Otto snapped, and flashed a look behind him. The MPs were following them in and the two in the rear of the jeep were already beginning to loosen their pistols in the leather holsters. He gulped. Now his nerves were tingling electrically, his heart beating like a trip-hammer.

'*Champ de tir*,' the Count noted, pointing to the faded wooden sign to their left. 'That means shooting range,' he translated, without even a tremor.

'Shooting range!' Otto groaned. Then this was it. They were going to be bumped off, real Gestapo-style. 'Shot while trying to escape . . .' After all, they *were* enemy aliens.

'Comfort stop,' Cowen explained, using that absurd American euphemism, 'so you guys can go to the bathroom.' But Otto wasn't fooled. He noted the strained note in Cowen's voice. He had to do something – and do it soon.

'Why don't you say "have a piss"!' he roared crudely, and lashed out just as Cowen was reaching for the brake, gear in neutral.

The blow on the nose caught the new light colonel completely by surprise. Something snapped. Thick red blood began to spurt out immediately, and Cowen reeled back, howling. 'What the –'

Otto gave him a huge dig in the ribs and he flew out of the jeep, gobs of thick blood shooting everywhere, staining the snow. Otto hesitated no longer. He sprang into the vacant seat.

Behind him, a gruff voice commanded, 'Hold it there buddy!'

'What *are* you doing, Otto?' wailed the Count. 'I've been pressing my knees together for the last half hour!'

'Piss yerself!' Otto roared, fumbling with the gears, fingers trembling with excitement and fear. 'Grab that fire extinguisher. For Chrissake – *quick*!' Smashing home reverse, Otto floored the accelerator. The jeep shot backwards. Smack! It rammed the front of the jeep, sending the white mice fumbling wildly for their guns and falling all over the place.

'Use the fire extinguisher!' Otto yelled above their curses and excited cries. 'Spray the windscreen . . . *Los* . . . *Los*!'

Contrary to regulations, the MPs had been driving the jeep with the windscreen up. In combat zones, it was always supposed to be down. Now as they scrambled to right themselves and Cowan, holding his fractured beak, sat moaning in the pimpled snow, the Count thrust the brass plunger down. Thick white foam spurted from the extinguisher.

'Oh, I say, Otto, this *is* fun!' he chortled, like a child

with a new toy, merrily spraying the thick goo from one end of the windscreen to the other, his plump face wreathed in joy.

Otto flung one last glance behind him. It would take them a good few minutes to clear the white muck away, and he guessed the frost would make it difficult to undo the catches that held the windscreen upright.

'Hold tight, Count!' he yelled above the angry cries of the white mice, 'here we go!' He engaged first gear and pressed down hard on the accelerator. The jeep shot forward. With a snarl of brakes, a screech of protesting rubber, he was out of the quarry and back onto the *route nationale*.

'*Halt, or I'll fire*!' bellowed a white mouse.

'*Duck*!' Otto yelled wildly. Next moment they were off, careening crazily from one side of the road to the other, racing desperately for the next curve, the slugs howling harmlessly off the *pavé* on both sides.

Behind them, Lieutenant Colonel Cowen hugged his fractured nose, swaying back and forth and moaning miserably.

Although the day was far advanced, the long rays of the sinking sun were still visible over the rim of the darkened French forest, touching the tips of the tallest trees lightly and burnishing them a shimmering gold. From a distance it looked as if the trees had been on fire and were now burning out with a last gleam of phosphorescence. From the German side of the Rhine came the soft, mellow tone of church bells and a faint chorus of '*Stille Nacht . . . Heilige Nacht*.' It was Christmas Eve in Germany, and at that moment the war seemed a million miles away.

Stiffly Otto crawled out of the jeep. With an air of finality, he switched off the ignition. They were out of gas anyway, and they couldn't get the jeep over the river without being observed. Even on this dead front, where the reformed French Army and the German Army had stared at each other impotently for three months, there would still be a few sentries posted, and Otto was taking no more chances. For him, the war was over at last. He'd had a noseful of them all – his own people, the Tommies, the Amis, the Popovs, the Cheeseheads, the Spaghetti-eaters – the whole damned shoot!

'What now, Otto?' the Count asked softly, his glistening eyes fixed on the far bank of the river, with its cluster of white-painted cottages around an onion-domed church, covered with snow.

'What now?' Otto echoed, as he stared at the dreamy twilight coming from the east, limned in a thin frame of ochre and pink, like rocks rising abruptly from a pale-blue sea. 'Yes, what indeed, Count?' And he shrugged a little helplessly, as if he had come to the end of his wisdom.

The Count seized his opportunity. 'Don't despair, my boy!' he declared, swinging his right arm out from his breast dramatically. 'The day will surely come soon, when man, grown tired of venting his wrath on his fellow man, will turn to him as if to a brother. That day, when we have learned to feel the sorrows and the joys, the suffering and the hope of others as if they were our own, we shall know a world order of love and justice – that order for which the universe yearns and of which the planets in the silent heavens are the splendid but imperfect mirror . . .'

Otto gazed in amazement at this sudden outburst, but the Count hadn't finished yet. Thrusting out his bold chin, eyes blazing, he went on: 'On *that* day alone, the brotherhood of man will have become reality, Otto!' he breathed fervently, '*Man will love man*!'

'*Qui est là*?'

The challenge cut surprisingly into the Count's panegyric, as he poised there, arm outflung, chest heaving with emotion.

Otto swung round. A small man in the ragged uniform of the French Army stood at the edge of the trees, rifle raised uncertainly. In the background, more French soldiers could be seen emerging from the trees.

'Frogs,' Otto yelled. 'Hoof it, Count . . . *Schnell*!'

Just as the first dry crack of rifle fire broke the grand silence of that pastoral Christmas scene, the two fugitives plunged down the path that led to the Rhine and the Reich.

'*Man will love man – my arse*!' Otto snorted, and then he was gone.

It was Christmas Eve in the year of Our Lord, 1944, and Otto Stahl was running yet again . . .

Afterword

It is said that in the remotest corner of the great US Army's military prison at Leavenworth, a chain-gang still works every day from dawn to dusk. Their tasks are twofold, it is reliably reported by those who should know. One month, they prepare a stretch of macadam road to the rear of their own special cell-block; the next, they break it up again with their sledgehammers. Month after month, year after year, decade after decade, always the same two jobs.

All day long can be heard the sound of picks and shovels striking into the hard stone; the air is full of the stink of tar, the hard sunlight, the smell of male sweat and cheap tobacco. But there is singing, too: the kind of singing one might have heard forty years ago in the Deep South, or in those US ghetto synagogues, where the cantors were not native-born but had come from Eastern Europe, instead of being the budding Dean Martins they all seem to be these days.

Of course, the singing doesn't have the same body and volume it once had. After all, most of the chain-gang are in their seventies now, and there aren't as many of them as there used to be. Yet still their singing has something of the old power – that power that can make the listener's heart beat faster or cause him to grow cold with ecstasy and fright.

Even the oldest of their guards, who still tote sawn-off shotguns and wear pistols at their hips (though none of the chain-gang are strong enough to make a break for it now), do not know what their crime is, or how they ever even got to Leavenworth in the first place. If the prisoners themselves ever knew why, they have long forgotten. All that is known is that they are 'lifers' with no hope of a pardon – a decision which has been upheld by every successive President (for the President of the United States is, also, the Commander in Chief of the US Army) since the days of President Roosevelt. The men of the Leavenworth chain-gang will die behind bars.

What kind of gang *is* this, then, that can make such music? Well, they're just ordinary mortals – and all of them are black, save one; a runty little fellow with a swarthy face who is sometimes heard to mumble in his dotage that once, long ago, he was a light colonel of the Army of the 'good ole US of A' – a remark which provokes peals of laughter from his constant companion, a white-haired old buffer who looks the very picture of old Uncle Tom, though for some strange reason, the others call him 'Big Nig' . . .

OTTO AND THE YANKS

Leo Kessler

Volume four of the extraordinary memoirs of Otto Stahl – Casanova and conman supreme – and his eccentric, monocled best mate, The Count.

It is 1943 and the infamous duo find themselves recruited by General Patton himself for US Counter Intelligence. They are to play a crucial part in the Allied Invasion of Sicily. But there is more to this invasion than meets the eye. For far from being allies Generals Patton and Montgomery are archrivals competing for personal glory.

Believe it? Read on and find out as Otto and The Count talk their way out of sticky situations, blunder through hilarious adventures and take their pick of the buxom Sicilian broads!

Futura Publications.
Fiction/V War
0 7088 23130